Can We Share?

A Sip of Chai with Some Crispy Tales!

Novel by

Amit Bimrot

REDGRAB books

redgrabbooks.com

Published By
Redgrab books Pvt. Ltd.
942, Mutthiganj, Prayagraj, 211003
www.redgrabbooks.com
contact@redgrabbooks.com

First published by Redgrab Books in 2022
Copyright © 2022 Redgrab Books Pvt. Ltd.

Copyright Text © 2022 Amit Bimrot
Printed and bound in India
Cover Design & Typesetting by Redgrab Books team

ISBN : 978-93-90944-29-3

Dedicated to my Parents & Teachers,

Thank you for your support, knowledge & life lessons.

ACKNOWLEDGEMENT

There is a long list of people who supported me on this journey, Thank you Shraddha Tiwari for helping me out to finish this book, Thank you for your lovely words & brilliant edit it wouldn't have been possible without your immense support & hard work.

Thank you Sarah Sebastian for your time & creative support. Your inputs into the stories The last letter, LIFT, Autowala and bhutiya Guys are impeccable. You helped me out to make them one of best ones.

Thank you chhaya for helping me out with edit on some of the important stories of this book, " bhasad" & "Cover Story"

Thank you Akshay kowe for helping me out with one of my favourite "shatranj" you equally deserve the credit for developing it.

Thank you Sumit Gupta for always been there as an senior and friend to help me out with all the difficulties during & post FTII, Thanks to my FTII batchmates Sanjay, Alok, Shashank & shwetabh for always been there to help. Ashok Bishnoi (rapperiya baalam) thank you for all the great learning memories over the years.

And thanks to my family, most of my stories & character comes from my personal life.

This book equally belongs to all of you.

PREFACE

When I was in my FTII first year, I had this thought to make short films & utilise the time. But I believe the biggest difficulty was what to write & how. I have thought about many things, but nothing hit me right to start. I was looking for that idea of motivation. One day l was watching some documentary in which ordinary people were doing ordinary things, which help the society in a larger perspective. How your small deeds can make big changes in someone's life & that person is HERO.

For me A hero doesn't need to be doing always extraordinary things. A Hero could be any person sharing food with a hungry kid, helping old age person crossing road, or just walking side by side of a girl unknowingly when she needs it. Heroism lies in simple things as well, which we never see or try to acknowledge. That's when I wrote my first thoughts on few simple deeds of heroism. Later, wrote few more ideas & those films got appreciation by the audiences. Family drama to romantic comedy. I kept going, toughest part was the starting point.

You won't find extraordinary suspense, drama or romance but yeah you are gonna find all those everyday simple moments which we either ignore or take it for granted. And won't even realise till you feel hungry, need someone's help to cross the road, or just wish "this is wrong time and place hope someone would have given me a company."

Like one of my stories Autowala & the proposal 2 different genre & class accounts for this simple emotions felt by you all in some way.

"Miss you buddy" is about the feeling when we leave our houses for studies & Job to another city, I have experienced that in 2008 when I left home.

"Lift" inspired from a real incident happened with friend. I found it really interesting. I took some creative liberty & created the story. One of my favourite alongside "the last letter"

"Bhasad" and "Bhutiya Guys" are two social satire comedies, But both explore the pro & cons of the social media. Both inspired from many youtube prank channels.

"Can we share" is one story where one character wants to share with someone about what he feels. I believe that's what my all stories wanted to convey. "Cover story" follows the same romantic genre from the book but the drama emphasis how to "move on" in life & why it's important .

"karoption" inspired from a real incident happened in delhi during a political setback event.

"Fitrat" is complete different from all above it has drama more fiction, its about a person's desire & how greed can destroy a person's life.

All are simple stories of everyday life, simple characters which we usually see around, their simple conflicts & resolution. I believe simple things are the most difficult to write, see, feel & elaborate. In the rush of daily expectations, we just forget to live simple moments. This is small book to read over a cup of tea just to realise what we are missing.

You might not like the taste of your cup of tea for a moment, But I am sure you gonna smile while reading or gonna feel the simple emotions of each story. & you might feel that last sip better by the end of the story.

Thank You

Amit Bimrot

Author, Actor & Director

Contents

THE LAST LETTER

I just shifted to this lovely city Pune. And being from Delhi, Pune is heaven for me, with pleasant weather and fresh air. The soothing feeling of breathing clean air while cool breeze caress me; ahh! I could get used to this. The culture and history of Pune always drew me to it and finally I too am a part of it. Probably the only thing that I crave is food. Being surrounded by all sorts of delicacies all the while, I miss my favorites. But I am trying the authentic food available here; opening myself to Pune. Recently I had the Pithhla & Bhakri and it felt great although I wouldn't dare compare it to my personal favorites rajma chawal and chole bhature.

I remember the first time I had to move out. It was during my college days when I shifted to hostel. How homesick I was! Only thing that kept me going was the tiny dreams a normal guy had. But that appears now to be in the distant past. Now I am away from home to work, and I am no longer homesick. I am an engineer in Infosys; yes I know what you think. What a boring job! But don't we all have obligations to fulfill? And this mixture of being happy and sad together, probably all the engineers would know. But to sleep knowing that I did not let the guy who did not give up, even when he wanted to run back home, makes me smile. And still the thought of why I no longer am homesick lingers in my mind. Did I grow up somewhere in the run? Or maybe I found multiple homes; in different people, in different places, in different food, in all the universe I am put in.

And the newest such home that I found is in Pune. My office is at Chandichawk; oh yeah! There is one here too. Near to my office I rented this perfect little apartment in a very welcoming society of Kothrud. It's just two weeks and already my life is beautiful. From the morning rush to office and all the hectic works, I come back to a peaceful sunset and warm coffee. And in the end to go to bed smiling and feeling content is all I wished for myself. Another reason universe conspired to give me happiness is my neighbor. I remember the first time I saw her. I came in Uber and reached down of my apartment. And there on the floor I'm staying, I saw the amazing lady, bathed in sunlight, surrounded by exotic plants and beautiful flowers. Her saree danced slowly with the wind and her hair touched her face with the rhythm. I took my luggage and went up. And to meet her in person, I rang the doorbell and waited. There she was; an absolute beauty; my dadi. Touching 65, she could still compete with all the women out there with her prettiest smile.

"Namaste Dadi"

"Hi Beta"

"I am your new neighbor. Just shifted"

" Oh. That is such a relief. Come inside. "

I saw her apartment. Everything was well arranged and perfect. I spoke to her for almost an hour. Every time her soothing voice entered my ears, peace rushed to my mind. And that is when I noticed the pictures hung on the wall. I saw her pictures taken from different parts of the world. I discovered that she has travelled enough and asked her about her family. She told me her son is living abroad with whom she too lived but came back because she knew where she belonged. I felt proud of her. To live a life on one's own terms even at that age, I wondered if I am as strong as her? I had to leave by then and while leaving she held my hand and asked me;

"beta would you keep an eye on the postman for me?"

"Sure Dadi."

And from that day, every alternate day, she would ask me the same question even though she did not share anything more. And I assumed she was old school and loved reading hand written letters. And that made me love her even more. I still write my diary using fountain pen and the smell of the ink, the way the paper looks, the stain on my hands after writing all fascinates me. And that trait of humans, to grow and yet remain rooted is something I am thankful of. But I am more thankful of the food dadi makes. She invites me for dinner mostly and lunch occasionally. She is one of the best cooks I have seen and even the simple daal chawal she makes feels like chole bhature. And the cook in her and the foodie in me is a perfect combo.

Gradually we also moved to other dimensions like teacher-student. I taught her how to use online apps for bills, grocery etc.

and now she is a pro at it though she needs help here and there. And the happiness in making her life better made my day content. The way she expressed her love to me was through food. I would be having a horrible day at work and without even telling anything, when I come, there would be my favorite food waiting for me. The only person who is more happier than me to know I am having good food is my Mom. I could feel her relief through phone calls hearing I had good food and I am healthy.

One day I sat in my balcony having coffee watching random videos on YouTube. And a food blog came to my notice and that is when it strike me. Dadi is an amazing cook and the world should know her talent. I ran to her but she denied initially. And my face became dull hearing her no and just for my happiness, she said yes. But after few days, she started enjoying it. To cook in front of camera, to give description, to talk to millions. She found happiness. And post my office hours, I sat down and did the editing, uploading and promotion works. Gradually our subscribers increased and we celebrated all the little milestones together. But more than anything, her happiness mattered to me. She was never in a better state from the day I met her.

And one day, celebrating our first million views with homemade date cake, she opened up a little about her family to me. She always avoided personal questions and I was surprised to hear about her past. She told me about her husband, Mr. Kulkarni who use to be a higher rank officer in Indian Army and it was with him that she travelled most of the country. She spoke about all the beautiful places vividly and it felt like I saw those places. I could feel the freezing snow of Himachal piercing my hands, I could feel the Dal lake taking my breath away, I could feel the white sand of Ladakh entering my shoes while run around; I could feel everything. She had a happening life. And the joy mixed with a stroke of sadness she had made me more closer to her. I knew she had been through a lot in her life and she is focusing only on the good. What are you dadi? I would call myself blessed to be half as good at heart as you.

One fine morning I was rushing to my office and I got awestruck seeing her. She was wearing a purple banarasi saree with green work and it highlighted her beauty much more. She came near me with her elegant smile and I couldn't resist saying;

"You look stunning dadi"

"Thank you beta."

"Where are you going dadi? You have a date today?" I teased her.

She laughed out loud and said,

"Oh no dear, it's uncle's birthday today. Come home early today. We have a small party. I'm making cake." And the entire time in my office all I could think about was the love she had for her husband. To love unconditionally even when far; how lucky he must have been. My heart wondered where is was all the while I was travelling back. I reached and opened the door to see dadi melting the chocolate to pour on the cake. The child in me went and licked the spoon and smiled at her. And like the last time when we spoke eating cake, she opened up to me again. Like a teenager falling in love, her eyes danced around every time she spoke about him. She told me about him, the food he likes, the places he was posted, the way he dressed everything. And finally she touched her earrings and played with it slowly.

"He gifted this. This was the last gift. But my favorites are still the letters he wote."

I couldn't hold myself back anymore. I wanted to know where he was.

"Where is he dadi?"

Finally after a small silence she replied softly,

"He is posted in Siachen. And I am waiting for his letter. I am waiting for him. I am waiting. " And with that I could see her breaking down. She rushed away from me to her bedroom. I couldn't leave. I sat there for a while and went to check on her. There she was in her reading chair, serene and calm. I went and sat down on the floor slowly pressing her feet.

"Dadi, I want to read those letters."

She was numb. She did not say a word while she walked towards the table drawer near her bed. She came back to me with a bunch of letters very safely kept. I took them and came back to my apartment. I read them, each one of them, word by word. And until then all I could think was how lucky Mr.Kulkarni is to have a wife who is madly in love with him. But after reading the letters I knew, he reciprocated it the same way or more. He too missed her while he stayed away and loved her unconditionally. It was evident from each letter.

Next day, I met dadi with a heavy heart. I couldn't talk much. I rushed to office to keep myself engaged so that I needn't remember about dadi and her misery. But all the while I felt a burden on my chest. I felt the urge to do something for her. Immediately I took my phone and texted all my friends in army and also in groups. I waited for them to respond and by that night I got details about him. Mr.Kulakrni was part of a troop that went missing in 1984 during the Siachen glacier capture. His body was not found and they all believe he was resting there. And along with these, I also came to know about the tradition army soldiers had. Because of the way of their work, they always knew, any moment could be their last. So they kept a letter in their pocket in case if something happens to them for their loved ones. And the mere thought of what he must have written for my dadi broke me. I couldn't hold my tears back. Their love deserved a better ending. She deserves closure. I wanted to give her that. I called my friend who was a senior journalist with the gift of copying handwriting and told him everything. He was happy to help. I met him and we together went to Delhi to meet the head of the battalion. We collected more information about the incident and we together read those letters again. The second time I read those letters, I was broken even more. I could feel an unwelcomed pain rushing to me.

I returned from Delhi back to dadi. Our life went back to the way it was. We cooked, we ate, we made videos and we were happy.

Few days later, I was going to office and saw dadi when I opened my door. She had tears in her eyes. Her small nose was red.

"Thank you beta." And then I saw the letter in her hands. She held them close to her chest. She hugged it. I fought with my tears to not fall. I hugged her. I couldn't say anything. I walked down the stairs almost crying. Getting inside the cab travelling to my office but somewhere I was glad knowing dadi got closure. But will I ever get it? How can I when I crave to know what was in the last letter?

But in the end all that matters is that, dadi received the last letter.

LIFT

Harish Bhogle, a 50yr old businessman was driving from Chandigarh to Delhi with his young son Kartik & a lovely Dalmatian pup, Cherry. Harish went to Chandigarh to adopt Cherry from a friend. It's early morning & they have to reach Delhi by 2:30 to catch the Rajdhani Express from Delhi to Mumbai. Harish booked a 1st class AC cabin for Kartik & Cherry and decided to travel by car to Jaipur for his business and then fly to Mumbai.

Harish is a genial and optimistic man with a charming personality. He started his career from scratch & achieved great heights with his hard work and perseverance. He is adventurous, great conversationalist and loves to drive.

Due to heavy traffic jam on the toll plaza of Delhi border, they started running out of time. Harish picked up the speed of the car and drove hell for leather, but they still reached Nizamuddin railway station 15 minutes late and missed the train.

Since Kartik has aerophobia, Harish makes some calls and

pulls some strings to get a ticket booked for the next train that arrives after 2 hours for his son. Kartik persists to come along with him but Harish won't take a risk on his son's health for such a long ride. Harish takes Cherry along with him.

While Harish was seeing off his son, a bearded man in his late 20's, carrying a laptop bag, was observing their activities closely for quite some time.

He reaches towards Harish & asks politely. "Hello sir, agar aap Dhaula Kuan side jaa rhe hai toh LIFT milegi, actually meri train miss ho gyi".

Harish takes a closer look at the stranger & takes him along. As soon as they leave the railway station, Harish asks him to carry Cherry's bag on his lap.

The stranger introduces himself as Shakib Ali. He works at a mobile shop. When he said that his village is around NH48- NH08 Mewat region, Harish casually agrees to drop him nearby his place. Harish isn't familiar with the place so he follows the route on google maps & also asks Ali to guide him as well.

He asks Ali about his region, food & agriculture. Ali replies while secretly glancing at Harish's belongings. He saw luxurious dresses & expensive food items for the pup which made him ruminate about "who splurges on a damn dog"!

Since they open up a little, Harish reveals that "Cherry is like a kid to me. It's a gift from a close one who is no more."

As their conversation started getting deeper, Harish shares setbacks from his personal and professional life very casually with a wide smile on his face. He told him how he lost his mother and then got divorced and then lost his ex-wife to cancer. He also tells about the mistakes he made in his past like opening a bar where people gambled and got drunk and many from the underworld came there too. He shared his personal philosophy about life and success, which was very different. It made Ali a little bit uncomfortable, however, he was fascinated by Harish's remarkable character and simplicity. He was influenced and perplexed, wondering "how can someone endure adversaries with a smile and live his life so beautifully!" He couldn't believe that people like Harish 'actually' exist in this brutal world. Ali was born in Husainpur village of Mewat into an ordinary farmer family. Youngest of 3 brothers. Always been a brilliant student. Life changed upside down when he was in 12thstd. A family land dispute turned violent and he lost his father & eldest brother in the shootout. The other side of the family was financially stable so they grabbed their land and nothing happened to them. His mother fought the case over the years and died of heartache. This made Shakib took the responsibilities alongside his brother & grandmother. Have done all hardworking odd jobs like in cloth factory, construction, farming, mobile shop etc. He married at a young age. When brother was diagnosed with cancer unfortunately, he came under a huge debt. That moment pushed him into the crime world. Things started out turning to be so bad that now he needs big chunk of money for some important surgeries of his brother, for which he can do anything or go to any extent.

Harish & Ali took a few halts during their journey. It is nigh time as they left Delhi at sunset. They stop by a Dhabha, where Harish feeds Cherry and then orders dinner for them. Ali denies him initially but eventually joins him.

After a while, Ali's phone started ringing incessantly. He was getting some calls 'back-to-back'. He picked up a few calls in private. It appeared that the caller was screaming at him from the other side. Ali panicked after the call. While observing the stressed expressions on his face, Harish asks Ali, "what happened." Confused Ali lies to him saying, "Sir, Bhai ki tabiyat kaafi kharab hai. Mai jaake hospital le jaunga, paiso ki pareshani bhi hai".

Harish takes a moment to clear the bill, he takes out some cash and his visiting card and gives it to Ali. He says, "Rakh lo beta, meri koi madad lage toh batana". Ali tries to deny it but accepts it when Harish with a warm smile says, "I have recently lost someone very close to me. He could not receive adequate medical treatment on time. I don't want anyone else to suffer the same ". Ali went in a state of shock. He was stupefied by this gesture.

When they reach the car, a Police officer on regular duty arrives and asks Harish to show his ID and gives a suspicious glance to Ali which he tries to avoid. Harish asks Ali to take out the ID from the front pocket of the bag on the back seat of the car. While searching for the ID he finds another bag containing a stack of money which Harish was carrying for business purposes.

Ali returns to the front seat and shows the ID to the police officer and they leave. As they were about to reach his drop location, Ali's phone started ringing incessantly again but he hangs up the phone this time. Harish says "Beta, maa ka phone ho toh utha lo, issey badi luxury life mai kuch nai hai". A bit emotional & terrified Ali says, "Sir, idhar se muje jana hai, vaise yeh rasta aage

NH08 connect hoga aapka time bach jayga agar yaha se jaoge toh".

Harish drives towards an isolated road. The formation of fog interferes with visibility. Winter night fog almost covered the view. Harish is sceptical and asks Ali if the road connects to the other side. Ali gets many opportunities to kill but he can't. Suddenly, they see a bike accident on the road. A man was lying on the ground and a woman with a kid gesticulates them to stop the car. Ali started sweating in a bewildered state of mind. When surprised Harish stops the car, Ali holds Cherry close to his arms instantly & screams, "Sir, gadi bhagao."

Suddenly, their car was surrounded by three-four masked men armed with lathis. They were trying to harm them, breaking the windows and were continuously hitting the car with eggs on the windshield. They were abusing and shouting, "gate kholo". Ali instantly screams, "sir, gate band rakhna, gaadi chada do, wiper mat chalana". The scared pup started barking at the goons in a feeble voice.

Harish valiantly tries to find space to accelerate the car & succeeds in it. The car picks up the speed and leaves the goons behind. Ali warns Harish saying, "Sir, aage kile padi hongi road k niche se lena, abhi aage aur bhi bandey hai bike par, car mat rokna".

It happened exactly as he said it would be. Though they were able to dodge a few hurdles, they were in a tight spot. A few bikers started chasing them. They broke all the windows of the car with lathis. Ali was hit with a lathi on the head which caused injuries and a few shattered pieces of glass penetrated his ribs. Bleeding profusely, he held Cherry in his arm while trying to remove the cracked windshield of the car by his leg for better visibility.

Harish is injured a bit. Speeding up the car they could finally leave the goons far behind and catch a glimpse of NH08. While trembling and breathing heavily, they looked for a safe place to stop the car. To their relief, they saw a petrol pump nearby and pulled over the car. Harish came out of the car with a water bottle to wash Ali's wounds. He observed that Ali was bleeding while holding Cherry safely in his arms. Harish provides immediate first-aid to Ali and calls the ambulance.

Harish thanks Ali for risking his life to save him and Cherry. Ali breaks down and apologizes to him because he was the one who conspired with the goons to rob him and following him from Delhi was a part of his plan. He tells him that he would not allow them to hurt Harish even if they took revenge on him. Ali asks Harish why he trusted him when the police came and that is when Harish tells him that his son died while he was 10 minutes away from him in a road accident. The police took him to a hospital and all the money was of no use and helping he said gives him peace.

Though he had done some robberies in his past, it was for the first time he was plotting something that might take a life. And that too for financial help for his brother's treatment. Those vicious people could have done anything to Harish, which Ali's heart won't allow. Ali asks Harish "Sir, aap abhi safe hai aage Manesar town mai ruk jaye car thik karke phir niklein, mai chala jaunga yaha se don't worry."

Harish "Beta, tumhari halat thik nahi hai. LIFT mangi thi tumne toh ghar tak chodna padega". Meanwhile, a PCR van & an ambulance arrives to treat both of them. Harish calls his friends in Police department.

It's an early foggy winter morning in Ali's village in the Mewat region. His mother is feeding the livestock. A dented EcoSport car (wreaked car), with all the window glasses shattered, arrives at the vicinity followed by a PCR. Harish meets Ali's family and assures them that they will come to no harm and police will nab the culprits. Before leaving, Harish gives a bag containing money to Ali. Meanwhile, Cherry playing around. Both leave for Jaipur.

KAROPTION

An office scene opens up with a young boy sitting in an office arguing to an municipal officer, who is busy flattering the pages of the file.

I always thought the government works are easily done, until I came in contact with this fellow being at an municipal corporation office, I went as to request to get a pillar allocated at my locality.

The JE at the office told me to talk to harpal for the same, as I have been coming from last 4 days here, sir he is asking for 2000/- rupees, and why should I give this amount when I have already given the nominal charges for the work to be done.

JE - ' It won't be possible as the staffm members are on leave for 20 days.

Sir, I did talk to the people there, they are saying they are free and until you sign the documents, they won't be doing the work, okay sir, meaning I have to bribe you to have my work done.

JE in a loud voice told me to go, as if I was the one asking fir money.

I went to harpal again but he again demanded 2000/- rupees

for the work to proceed, but I refused.

I was in a state of shock and disappointed at the same time, my image crashed to see such corrupted people working in government offices, frustrated about the event I started to think whom can I call for this and share and take help from, just when I thought of a friend who belongs from such background.

Leaving the office I called my friend shivam and told him about the whole situation, when shivam advices to give the money to them. The following day I went back, telling JE that the amount has been given and to proceed with the work further. JE comments to me for my attitude earlier and tries to make me understand that these are the procedure and this is how you get the work done here.

I requested him to start the work.

JE replies – 'U should have done this before won't have wasted these 15 days.

(A group of people entered the office) CBI officials

Taking JE into custody and asking questions as I sat out waiting for the response from the people, remembering the advice Shivam has given me to record the corruptive act of JE from the camera of my mobile phone while giving him the amount, just when an officer approached me telling me that they will telecast the video tomorrow, thanking me for reporting this act. I told shivam about everything I have been going through from past 5 days and how his advice really worked against all odds.

It's this responsibility that makes us apart and fight for the wrongs in our country, the choice we make the option we have to make a change.

KEEP IT SIMPLE

That decision from your life which made you think deeply, any important thing which gets you thinking about all the doubts, the second thoughts, life gives us such questions. Deeply lost in her thoughts her friend comes up with a cup of coffee and a question asking about her decision regarding marriage, which still she haven't thought much about, her friend, 'if you still looking for the right person for yourself you can tell me, she taps his hand and tells him to stop, telling him that he knows he is perfect for her, but she is confused if this is the right time for her as her career is also lined up and after getting married makes priorities change so, diverting from the topic he asks her about the coffee, and helps her in figuring out by giving her a simple example pointing out the scenery out the window and telling her that just as she liked it without giving it much thought similarly she has to decide about this as well. With a smile she comments with a keen look towards him, 'okay mister gyan'

He shares some past memories with her to make her remember

all the incredible time she had, ' hey you remember the time we went to Shimla, it was a sudden decision but was full of surprise you remember'

The girl looks at him with an nostalgic feeling, and starts to laugh, ' do you remember the time when you lost your ticket and had to walk all the way to Ridge road..'

He gives her a annoyed look and starts to laugh himself, remembering these incidences that happened with them together, he notices her smile and looks away.

By the way what happened to your ladakh trip? he begins to explain her that he himself is confused about the trip, as he do wants to go but don't know' just then she points out the tree outside the window and tells him to look towards it, looking at it he remembers the trick she is about to play as he did, they both laugh at this drinking their coffee.

Somethings are meant to be simple and innocent instead of making it complicated with relationship it's the same…having a light hearted conversation is what makes it worth it.

Relationships are fostered by memories along the way, we just need to cherish it every moment.

BHUTIYA GUYS

Ali, Feroz and Bunty have been best of friends for as long as they can remember. Staying nearby in the small town, Malakhera of Alwar, Rajasthan, they went to school together. And even after studies, instead of going their separate ways like most did, they decided to stay. They knew nothing would give them more happiness than their hometown and each other's company. Now Bunty runs a Gym, Ali has a mobile shop and Firoz looks after the family dairy business. Everyday, before getting into their daily chores, it was their practice to have tea and kachori together from Mansingh's tea stall. The morning meetings were the energy drink they needed to meet daily difficulties. And that day, Ali and Feroz waited for Bunty wondering why he is late. It was then they saw Bunty running towards them.

"Listen! Last night some animal attacked our compound. Bapu thinks it is some bhoot and now we are all going to Sayyad Baba's place." Bunty was out of breath because of laughing and running. His voice echoed through the foggy roads of Malakhera.

Ali and Feroz too joined him laughing hearing how his family was scared to death believing some ghost is roaming around their home. Mansingh, who was hearing their conversation expressed his genuine concern through his perplexed face. The three youngsters were not just his customers; they were more than that. And that was the beauty of Mewat; they weren't large in number, but the small Meo Muslim community who lived there, lived in harmony loving and caring for each other.

"Beta, you should not laugh at Sayyad baba. He heals people with a mere touch. Please go and meet him before anything bad happens" Mansingh said to them humbly. The three immediately stopped laughing out of respect and walked away. Bunty was reluctant to go in the beginning but the three decided to go and have fun together. They reached the place around noon along with Bunty's family. There they saw a man in his 60's with long beard wearing white clothes hitting one by one with a magnificent sword claiming to be healing them. Ali was the first one to burst out laughing and the other two joined. The whole scenario appeared to be extremely funny to them and just like they planned, they were having fun. And in between the random sarcastic comments, an idea popped in Ali's head.

"Guys, listen. Why don't we recreate this and upload on YouTube?"

"Yes! It's going to be real fun. Look at all these people. They really believe in all this." Firoz replied to Ali.

The next weekend, they came together in a deserted place and recreated "paranormal" activities in a humorous way. Firoz became the reporter who interviews Ali who is the bhoot, who roams around shattering everything he sees like an animal. All the other actors around makes fun of the bhoot for doing such meaningless things. The group, even while shooting has fun and uploads it on their newly created YouTube channel *Bhootiya Guys*. The local people were initially offended and many of them tried to stop the three. But gradually, their videos got viral and more and more people started enjoying it. People even started commenting about the haunted places there know, asking the *Bhootiya Guys* to go shoot an episode there. And eventually, they started earning money through YouTube and sponsorships and the locals too started supporting them. People appreciated their bravery and the three earned a name not only in their locality, but also in other towns.

An year passed since they uploaded their first video and they came together at Bunty's home for celebrating it. They invited all their close friends and family and gave them a party. That is when Ali's maternal aunt, Raheema, tells them about the "Bhoot ki Bawadi".

"It is not like all those places you went before. This is really haunted. Please don't go there my kid. That woman would not leave you." Raheema said lowering her voice in fear. Immediately, they get inspired and the next day itself they go visit the place. The three plans yet another sarcastic episode where Bunty would play the woman in full-on haunting attire. They waited for two days for the full moon to get moonlit shots of the place for creating more impact. And finally, the day came and they place the cameras at two different angles and waited for Bunty's entrance. Bunty comes and he doesn't do things as planned and many times went out of the frame too. Ali and Firoz shouts in between but was impressed by his performance. When they were about to say cut, Ali's phone starts ringing and it was Bunty. Thinking Bunty lost his phone and someone is trying to give it back, Ali attends the call,

"Ali, I'm really sorry. I will reach in 20 minutes. I couldn't find the right size Lehenga."

Ali couldn't more or speak. He was shocked to core and whispered what happened to Firoz. Firoz looked around in search of who it was then they mistook for Bunty.

"Who the hell was it Ali?" Firoz yelled. Ali held is hands tightly unable to talk.

And then, a dark haunted faced woman appeared wearing a red chunri. Her feet were floating on air and seeing that, the two screamed at the top of their voice. They cried for help but no one lived near that place because it was haunted. They knelt down and apologized to her. And that was when Bunty came running fully dressed to play the ghost. He was shocked to see Ali and Firoz on the ground and a woman in front of them. The woman shrieked at him and Bunty and he too joined the two asking her forgiveness.

They tried running but their bodies were numb. Firoz somehow managed to get up and he thought maybe deleting the videos they took might help. But every time he tried to delete, the woman would scream and he would fall back. Ali seeing all this was scared to death and started crying like a baby. And instead of deleting, Firoz ends up shooting everything. Finally exhausted and out of breath, the three would hug each other and sit down in front of her. She in all the might would tell them,

"Not laughing anymore?"

"Please forgive us. We would do everything you ask for."

"Then you should show the world what happened today. Let them know we are real." She told in stern and scary voice.

The three agreed and ran away to home as soon as they could. All the three lost their sleep and started praying for courage. Next morning, they sat together and saw the videos again. Without any editing the uploaded all the videos to get peace from the woman. They were thinking about what their audience would think of them and if they would call them cowards. But nothing mattered more than getting rid of the woman. To their surprise, the audience thought even that was a created sarcastic video and supported it like before.

Unlike what they thought, the woman did not leave them. She took them to more and more haunted places. She made them shoot more episodes of them getting scared and made them upload everything. It was not the bhoot who was the joke anymore, it was the *Bhootiya Guys*. And all their audience believed it was all created for fun and supported them like before. Gradually, they started believing in everything they rejected. They started apologizing to their family and neighbors for mocking at them. They even went to the Sayyad Baba's place for his blessing. The entire life of the three changed.

And one morning, still worried about what to do, they were having tea at Mansingh's tea stall.

"I really hope she leaves us." Ali said sipping tea. And Firoz nodded his head and responded,

"I can't even sleep properly. We need to get rid of her."

"What more does she wants from us?" Bunty said a little louder desperately.

"Ask her." Said Mansingh.

The three turned in shock because they did not know Mansingh was hearing their conversation. They suddenly stopped talking.

Mansingh continued,

"Ask her what she wants. And tell her you don't want her in your life. Don't lie to her beta." Mansingh thought they wanted to get rid of some girl in their life and he who had a daughter was concerned about the girl getting hurt. So, he wanted them to tell her the truth and leave her with respect. The three who always did not pay much attention to his words that day listened to him. They directly went to the Bhoot ki Bawadi in search of her, without waiting for her to come. And to their surprise, the always scary woman was calm then. And though scared, they went close to her.

"We wanted to…" Ali stared talking and she interrupted him. She looked away from them and said,

"No one came." She took a pause and continued,

"No one came for me. I was coming back from Jagganath Mela. Suddenly something fell on the back of my head. I was hit. I saw my own blood coming out of my body. I was dragged. I smelled the red blood. And then I fell asleep. Pain was the last thing I knew."

She had tears in her eyes. The three who always saw her with fear, empathized with her.

"And then I woke up and saw my own body. I couldn't go back to it. I cried. I waited there for someone to come for me. No one did. I still lay there. Waiting."

The three could not move. They had tears in their eyes for her. They felt sorry for her. To go through all this alone. They did not say anything and went back.

They reached back and started searching for the girl who went missing at the Jagganath mela. They asked around everyone. And finally, it was Raheema aunty who told them,

"It was long back. From all the nearby villages these girls come. I met a group of girls in the morning during prayers. And in the evening, the same girls saw me and asked if they saw a girl in red chunri. I told I don't remember."

"You remember how this girl looked?" asked Ali.

"No beta. It was a few years back. I don't remember. No wait, she had a crescent moon shape mark on her right cheek."

The three stood up in shock with goosebumps. It was her. And they couldn't help but believe in fate, because the same Raheema aunty who told them about the place itself is telling about the girl. Maybe the universe is giving Raheema aunty a second chance to guide people near to the woman. The three immediately goes to see her.

"Hey." Bunty said to her.

"You came back?" she looked at them surprised. "No one comes back."

"You're wrong. They searched for you. They searched for you long. They couldn't find you."

She looked at Firoz earnestly with tears. She sighed out of relief knowing people wanted her. They did search for her. The pain she felt all these years started leaving her.

"Tell us where you're lying. Let us bury you. You deserve peace." Said Ali.

"She knelt down and cried covering her peace and they consoled her. They were no longer scared of her. They stayed with her until she stopped crying. She stood up in air again and lead the way silently. They walked for an hour but did not feel any pain in their legs. It was like even they were walking in air. They reached a desolate place and she stood there under a lonely babul tree. And she sat down it. The two without saying anything to each other started digging. And even that did not tire them. And one by one, they found her remaining. All the while, tears flowed from her eyes touching the crescent moon in her face. She did not know who or why she was murdered. But she forgave them. She blessed the culprits.

Ali, Firoz and Bunty gave her a burial with all the rituals. They were her family. They mourned for her and prayed for her soul. Without even knowing her name, or where she belonged, they cared for her. They turned back after the final prayers to see she had already gone. The bhoot left the Bhootiya Guys and they never went back to make any video. Next morning Mansingh asked them,

"You did not hurt her right?"

"No. She left." Said Ali.

"She found peace." Said Bunty.

They had tea in silence thinking about her wondering about the irony they are facing. The same woman they somehow wanted to get rid of finally left and they crave for a goodbye. The three went one last time to the "Bhoot ki Bawadi". They sat there and watched all the videos they made together. And then, Ali took the phone and deleted their account. And then they saw the crescent moon sending a breeze to them. And then they knew, it was her saying adieu.

AUTOWALA

Like always, the Nizamuddin Railway Station is crowded with busy people and Rajveer found it difficult to push them away to make his way. The train got delayed by an hour and he ran with time in his hands to the auto stand. He kept on saying sorry because he knew he was pushing and stamping many while running.

At this time, Usman was having tea which is also his breakfast. He was chatting to the tea stall keeper about the news he heard in his radio. Usman's eyes then fell on Rajveer and immediately his eyes got stuck. He went a little closer and heard his conversation with his fellow auto drivers.

"please bhayya, I'll give you 50 rupees. Please drop me"

Usman saw the negotiation happening and understood the young man has his SSC exam at DCAC college and needs to reach their before 10. Usman immediately hurries to him;

"I'll drop you beta. Come."

"Thank you so much uncle." And Rajeev goes behind Usman with a relief. He enters the auto and suddenly his face gets a dull stroke seeing the tasbeeh near the handle. Rajveer got uncomfortable seeing them. He said to himself that he has no other option so to travel with him.

Usman kept seeing his face through the rare view mirror. The face, the face of his son, Usman couldn't help but notice how similar they were. For helping him reach on time, Usman started taking all the short cuts he knew from his 32 years of being an auto driver.

Rajveer grabbed his bag tightly fearing the ways Usman is taking him. Every time he saw Usman looking at him through the mirror, Rajveer's heart rate paced. He prayed for the journey to end soon and give his exam and get home as early as he could. For diverting his mind from the fear, he opened his book and started going through the notes he made previous night. He prayed to his favorite little Krishna to help him somehow to reach there on-time safely. And to his surprise, he reached there on-time. He took out the money from his two different pockets and counted them carefully and that's when Usman stopped him gently touching his fingers. Rajveer immediately pulled back his hands and for a brief moment they looked at each other.

"Beta, jalti andar jao. Main rahoonga idhar. Exam ache se dena". Rajveer though wanted to send him back, couldn't waste time arguing. He rushed inside and that's when he realized he had forgot his pen. He cursed himself and ran back to meet Usman hallway, sweating and panting.

"Beta, you forgot your pen."

"Thank you, uncle."

Rajveer went inside and with all dedication and concentration, wrote his first round. When he came out for the lunch break, he saw almost every candidate with someone close, their parents, friends, or relatives. He saw them all waiting with food and water, asking how the exam went. He went near a watchman to ask him where he could find some cheap lunch. Rajveer missed his mother and he took his phone to call her, when Usman patted on his shoulder.

"Beta, how was your exam?"

"Oh, it went good."

"Come let's have lunch. I asked the watchman there and he told me when you would come. The biriyani here is good. Let's go to that park nearby and eat in peace."

"You shouldn't have bothered." Rajveer said coldly.

"No beta. You should eat. When you're hungry, you won't be able to concentrate for your exam. Come, let's eat."

Rajveer though hesitant, went with Usman because he indeed was very hungry. Inorder to board the train on time, he did not even wait to eat breakfast and all he had was tea while travelling. Rajveer saw two different packets in Usman's hand and wondered why he brought food from two different shops.

"Beta, this is veg and this is non-veg. I didn't know what you would prefer."

Rajveer was awestruck with the effort Usman took for him. And somewhere he also doubted the intentions.

"I'm a non-vegetarian."

They ate food in silence with brief eye contact in between. Usman did not leave a single chance to see his face.

"You remind me of my son beta."

"Oh."

"Who all are there in your family?"

"My mother and me."

Rajveer got up and cleaned his hands with the water left in his bottle. Immediately Usman got up and told him to wait there and left with the bottle. Rajveer saw him going to a nearby shop and the waiter there filled the bottle and gave it back. Rajveer understood that everyone there knew Usman and they were very affectionate towards him. He brought a smile in everyone with his charm and enthusiasm. This made Rajveer calm a little more. He took back the water bottle and said,

"Thank you for everything. Please go and do your job. I will manage."

"Job will be there tomorrow also beta. You are new here. Some auto drivers will misguide you. Don't think about all this now. Go and write your exam well. Allah will guide you."

Rajveer went to give his second round with a filled heart and stomach. He gave his best and was content. After the second round, unlike before, Rajveer came by himself to Usman without much thought, even he was surprised by the way he was somewhere liking Usman.

"My exam went really good Uncle. Thank you so much. I can't tell you how indebted I am to you."

"Don't be beta. May you get good marks. Come let's go and catch the return train. Your mother must be waiting."

"Oh God. I forgot to call her."

"Call her whenever you can. You never know when is the last chance you get."

Rajveer looked and Usman's eyes and he saw the reflection of a pain running through him- the person always smiling. Rajveer stepped aside and called his mother. He told her about Usman and everything he did for him. While Rajveer was talking over phone,

Usman kept looking at him. The way he walked, the way he smiled, the way he talked, everything was cherished by Usman.

"Let's go?"

"Yeah beta, come."

Rajveer got into Usman's auto again. This time he sat back relaxed and noticed the white pearls of the tasbeeh. Unlike before, he felt peace. He laid back and closed his eyes without looking the roads through which they were going. He knew, Usman would take him safely to his destination. Usman this time did not take any short cut. He wanted to stay longer with the young man that reminded him about his son. They reached the railway station and Usman gently rubbed his hands through the forehead of Rajveer;

"Beta..."

Rajveer woke up and smiled,

"Reached?"

Rajveer got out of the auto and took all the money he had and offered it to Usman.

"Uncle please give me your account details, or do you have Google pay? I'll send you money as soon as I reach home."

Usman refused to take the money and took his hand and slowly patted Rajveer's head as if he was blessing him and said,

"Come back and ask for Usman, the autowala, once you get job. And then you can pay me back. Now go home."

"Why!?" Rajveer almost exclaimed unbelievably in the goodness of Usman's soul. He wanted to know what made Usman do all this for him, a complete stranger. He looked at Usman earnestly waiting for an answer. After taking a deep breath, with a pain clouding his eyes, but still smiling, Usman spoke in low voice,

"My son looked just like you. Even he wanted to be an officer like you."

"Wanted? He doesn't dream about being an officer now?"

"He is no more to dream."

Rajveer was taken aback. He did not know what to say to console this man who lost his son. He held his hands tightly. Usman looked away unable to face Rajveer and continued,

"It was five year back, in our Muzzfarpur village. Some kids of your age wrote something in that..what is it called? Facebook. And there was a communal riot near our home and my wife had gone out to buy vegetables. Our son went in search for her and we lost him instead."

Usman took a deep breath and rubbed his face.

"Beta, study more. Learn about everything. And then maybe you will be able to see us. See us as humans. Without any labels. Study as long as you see humans in every human you see."

Rajveer hugged Usman tightly and turned back and suddenly walked away. He sat alone in a bench in the Delhi Railway station. He closed his eyes. He walked back five years.

It was an early morning. He sat with his fellow party members in his classroom. He was a graduate student involved in heart core right wing politics. UP elections were coming up and made a fake video to spread hatred so that the Muslim candidates would lose. He uploaded that in his Facebook page saying how Muslims invaded our country and they are hurting Hindus in multiple ways. And later on, they celebrated the victory of the right wing without knowing the irreversible damages they have caused.

Now years passed, he is trying to get back in life. Rajveer realized nothing and no one can help him feed himself and his family. The exam was his last attempt before getting age over. And the reason behind him writing the exam well was the person who lost his son because of the momentary revenge he wanted to take.

Rajveer realized what he had done. He could sense a severe pain rushing to his chest. Tears flowed from his eyes, he felt it hard to breath. He had an emotional break down. Rajveer cried for hours. He didn't even realize the last train to his home had left. He fell asleep crying in the station. It was past midnight when he woke up. His eyes felt heavy and head dizzy. He took out his phone and opened his Facebook page. He saw how many of them reposted it and the hatred spread because of him. He deleted the post he wrote 5 years back and wrote another one, dedicated to lives lost in Muzzfarpur village riot titled,

Tasbeeh of Usman- the autowaala.

ONLINE WAR

It was just like some regular evening two friends sitting together each one with their mobile phones taking about some video eating and sharing each other the social media's updates and videos when they talk about some army video and comments on it, while arguing and telling each other how they are gonna fight through their words on social media, just when their third friend who was doing the dishes notices them aggressive and with hatred in their voices, they are superficially talking about the war and how they will bring most people down it they went on fields themselves.

Listening to this Sameer's eyes filled with tears while doing the dishes, as he remembered about his close cousin who died on the field and sacrificed his life for the nation, all his emotions about the war and his brother filled his mind and he went to them saying, 'You guys are making fun and think this is an easy situation to be in, not knowing what people go through there, you should not comment on the thing when you do not know anything about it' 'the people who are going through the things right now know what to do with it, you people don't have to sit here on internet and make the situation worse thought your words and start an online war'

Listening to this his friends became serious asking about his cause of concern regarding this, 'hey, why are you getting angry and serious bro, we are just trying to chill out here'

Sameer, 'I lost my closest cousin in the war, he fought through some toughest times there'

I know how all this looks from outside and what it really is on an inside, man.

Hearing to this his friends apologised to him saying, ' we didn't knew, we are sorry for such an act and comments' we get what you are trying to convey.

Thanks man,

They share a brotherly gesture hugging each other and sharing Diwali sweets.

Our military and saviour are doing their jobs perfectly as they should we should be grateful enough to respect it without making it more complex for them to handle it. Share a smile and love in your life.

MISS YOU BUDDY

Don't we all have that one person in our life; to whom we run to, the moment something happens? To whom we share the joys and sorrows of our lives? Who is our confidante and our home? Well for me it is my little brother Golu. I still remember the day he was born. I was a 6-year-old kid when me and papa waited outside the labor ward of Civil Hospital. I came directly from school in my uniform and waited for "her" like my papa told me. And then a beautiful nurse with round face and flawless dusky skin came with a white wrap. Me and papa ran towards the nurse and surprising us, *he* came. And from that day onwards, I have not felt alone. No matter what happened in my life, who I become, what I do, I knew he would love me unconditionally.

And never living apart from each, now I have to leave for work. That too to the other side of the globe, America. My heart aches to know I wouldn't be coming back to him every night. I tried to focus on my work keeping my eyes on the laptop and Golu enters,

"Bhaai, keep this. It is going to be cold there. I called Kiran and asked about his brother there."

I looked up and saw it was his favorite jacket. I felt a pain deep in me. I couldn't risk crying in front of him and I tried to avoid eye contact with him.

"I am busy Golu. I need to send this email before evening. Give that jacket to mamma. She is packing there."

I could see Golu turning away disappointed because he wanted to have a conversation with me. I finished my work and gathered all my inner strength and went to him.

"Golu, come, let's play."

Immediately his face lights up and he takes the chess board and arranges everything. The day I taught him how to play came to my mind. How many questions he asked me! And then the first time my Golu beat me; how proud I was. Will he ever know what he means to me? And then making his best move waiting for me to play, he said to me,

"With whom will I play chess from tomorrow bhaai!"

I chose not to answer that and pretended to focus on the game. Fluffy, our pet dog, who usually plays around Golu's feet was not leaving me then. Did she understood I am leaving? Why else would she come closer to me? Multiple thoughts lingered in my mind. More than anything, my mind was praying that Golu shouldn't ask if I would come for Diwali. How will I be able to tell him I signed a year contract and won't come before that. Golu like always read my face and in order to change the topic, he said,

"When did you start smoking bhaai?"

I was shocked. He knew! I always tried to hide it from him because of three reasons. I was ashamed of it, I didn't want him to smoke, and third reason being the most important- I would lose the right to stop him from smoking. And now that I know he knows, all I am bothered is about him even accidently telling it to mamma. I am leaving to another country for work and I am still scared of my mother. Do we ever become grown ups for them? But I don't want to be one. I still enjoy her coming and patting my head every time she is proud of me, I love the way she shouts my name every time I forget to wash my tiffin box, I enjoy the days I am tired and she feeds me with her own hands. And I would never want her to know her son is a grown up now. That he smokes, he drinks, he has a girlfriend and what not! At least not now. Maybe later sometime I would tell her myself.

"Golu, you know?"

"Of course I know bhaai. I am not as dumb as you think I am."

"Mamma knows?"

"Definitely not!" Golu yelled.

"Between us?" I winked at him. Every time we shared something that is to be kept between us, we say this to each other.

"Remember the first "between us" bhaai?"

And we laughed out loud. It was during my tenth grade a Christmas time. Papa's friends were Christians and they came with vine. Mamma kept in the kitchen and I desperately wanted to try it. I waited for Abba and mamma to leave the home in my charge. And then a weekend came and they went for a party leaving me and Golu at home. Golu was in his sixth grade and I helped him with his studies and gave hime some math sums to do and came to the kitchen. I grabbed the vine bottle and poured a little to the glass. I drank it and kept the bottle back. I turned back to leave and saw Golu standing there. I was scared to death at that moment and all my little munchkin asked was,

"It tastes good bhaai?"

"Not that good Golu. Don't tell anyone okay?"

"Between us."

"Between us." And we gave a hi-fi then. Years passed now. Somethings never change though. And that's when I noticed it was already late for us to have dinner. We went inside and Golu couldn't stop talking. He has a friend whose brother too left for work to U S and Golu collected all the details. I knew he was getting emotional and I stopped him and put him to sleep. And before I left, he asked me,

"What about bhabi bhaai? How will you two meet? Even calling would be difficult right?"

His questions somewhere annoyed me too. He was becoming my mamma and Papa.

"Just sleep Golu. We need to wake up early morning."

Next morning when I wake up, Golu is already at the breakfast table. I went and sat near him and poured coffee.

"Bhaai, I don't want a smartphone."

I was shocked to hear him say that out of nowhere.

"I will get good grades. I will get admission there. I asked Kiran and his brother. I will really work hard bhaai."

I couldn't say anything back. I was overwhelmed with his words. He would work harder just to be with me. How blessed I am. I don't say anything back to him and he gets annoyed and pretend to throw water on my laptop. I take my laptop away and finishes my works.

Finally, the hour for me to leave came. All the memories I have of my home, came running to my mind. From the mornings I spend in kitchen with mamma to the night I roam around with Golu, from the evening strolls with fluffy to the news debate with Papa, all my special daily moments came running to my mind. I convinced myself one year would pass soon and said goodbye to all heavy heartedly. I forbade them coming to airport because I wanted the last image of them the in my home and not in the airport crying. I took an Uber and as soon as I reached the airport I video called Golu in mamma's phone.

"Golu, go to the cupboard where we keep the chess board."

"What is it bhaai?"

"Go and see."

He goes and takes the perfectly packed yellow gift. He opens it and looks at me with tears.

"You will get good marks even with smartphone. And how can I sleep without seeing you Golu?"

We both cried. We both smiled. And like forever, we knew we would be together.

Bhasad (Mess ups)

A massive crowd on this miraculous day of the YouTube fest 2021 where all our leads come up on the stage waving their hands, they have their channel of 30 million and a hug fan base, with so amazing audience. The press starts with asking the journey and how it all came to this..?

The guys starts, here's how it all begun,

This is no ordinary story of three crazy friends! It's a series of real-life incidents. It is an adventurous journey of our three weirdos who come from different societal backgrounds. let me introduce you to the trio.

Sahil is a sincere, hardworking, ambitious, wannabe Entrepreneur who dreams to establish a startup company - noble intentions!

He has two friends, (Ranjan and Vicky) Who according to him are completely wasted and are a bad influence. He thinks that they don't have the drive and seriousness in comparison to his tenacity and ambition. He keeps on mumbling that he is not going to participate in the escapades of the two dumbheads but always ends up doing the complete opposite. /joining them.

Ranjan as the name suggests is always indulged in enjoyment. He is only into having fun and enjoying life. He is a son of a wealthy businessman. Yet, he chose to drive Maruti 800 over any other car! Such a weirdo! Though he has a lots of contacts, he never manages to get them in use!

Vicky is an aspiring actor. He flunked his college once. And is repeating his degree through correspondence.

The trio shares an apartment in the suburbs of Delhi. Though they keep on showering abuses at each other constantly, they are truly 'three peas in a pod'. Sahil has to splash water on his friends (who 'sleeps like a dog' according to him) to wake them up. Their day begins with a quarrel (of course with each other) . Either Sahil would be scolding them for their inappropriate, immature behaviour or accusing them of all the troubles they have caused to him. He prefers his place to be immaculately clean and constantly chides them for making it a complete mess.

No matter how extensively they squabble with each other they always stand by each other.

They go to the same college. And attempts to cover up for each other. It's usually Sahil who ends up bailing them out and not vice versa. Vicky, Sahil and Ranjan share a deep friendship. Vicky trusts that Sahil will assist him in any predicament for he has obviously done it so many times in the past.

Sahil's girlfriend Shivani doesn't like the two lunatics whom he calls his friends. She can't stand them. Sahil's teachers also advise him to stay away from the two loiterers. They might cause a stain on his reputation.

After college, the trio would meet at the Humayun Makbara, like they used to meet in school days.

Everyday, Sahil would grumble how he always gets apprehended because of their ludicrous activities.

One day he shares his entrepreneurial idea of starting an online portal for antique products from rural India. The only dilemma was to acquire funds for his business to get started for the manifestation of his dream.

To which Vicky comes to rescue! He tells him that his father has some friends who are into investment and they might be interested in helping Sahil with his amazing startup idea. Vicky speaks to his father, who later shares the contact number of a businessman from Gurgaon. They call him to get an appointment for the next day.

On the day of the meeting the trio plan to reach the destination on foot! (Oblivious to the fact that it rained the previous night and the pothole-ridden roads were filled with muddy water.)

Sahil is embarrassed with the looks and company of Rajan because he didn't bother to take a shower or dress up properly for the very important meeting! As they moved a little bit further, a car splashes a muddy puddle on them.

Drenched by a bucketload of a filthy pool of water which

possibly also had sewer water mixed in it, Rajan and Vicky got infuriated & started hurling abuses at the car owner. Mr Srivastav comes out of the car and apologises for the inadvertent splashing by the driver and offers them a ride to clean up at his office. To which Rajan and Vicky get enraged and start having a verbal argument with Mr Srivastava who explains that there is no way to drive a four-wheeler in the rain without splashing some water. "Splashing was unavoidable on this road which is filled with potholes. This is bound to happen! Inadvertently! And you fools should have come prepared for it! How could you expect water not to splash! "

Enraged Rajan and Vickey started spewing insults at him. Sahil tries to handle the situation and respectfully asks Mr Srivastava to leave.

When they reached the meeting place they are dumbfounded to learn that the person they were supposed to meet was Mr Srivastava! They started apologising to him. To which he whispers it's okay and asks about their business idea. And if they would like to have a cup of tea or coffee. Rajan replies by saying that he would like to have lemonade with 2 tsp sugar and a pinch of rock salt.

Vicky quietly kicks his leg under the table and

Everyone shares an uncomfortable glance.

Sahil continues "No thanks sir, I'm good. The core idea is to sell rural antique designs & products online. In the market, retailers buy these products at very cheap rates and sell it at exorbitant prices; exploiting poor farmers and artists."

Rajan interrupts him by casually saying "It's kind of a social service."

Annoyed Sahil continues "No no sir it's not a SOCIAL SERVICE. In future, we can expand it by buying their raw crops at the best price and we can sell online or we can collaborate with the government and finish the mediators who always exploit poor farmers."

Mr Srivastava replied, "Your idea is as good as charity and it doesn't seem to be very profitable."

Sahil was about to reply but Ranjan interrupts him by saying "Ok then consider it a charity! Please! God will bless your poor soul! "

Mr.Srivastava gets annoyed and asks if this boy has gone nuts! He reiterated that he is not interested in the proposal.

Sahil has a lot more to say, but Mr.Shrivastav already started striding away.

Sahil thanks him for his valuable time and walks out disappointed.

The trio meets at Mc Donald's. Sahil is dejected with the series of events that have happened. He is reluctantMr talk to his friends. Vicky tries to convince him not to lose hope, they will figure out something and will find more contacts. Meanwhile, Ranjan is enjoying a burger unabashed by nothing and completely chilled out!

While Sahil was talking about how the puddle splash and silly conversation by the two morons ruined his chance, Ranjan points out to a fantastically wealthy-looking man approaching them. He was a well-dressed man flaunting his shining iPhone 12 pro.

Everything about him oozed out wealth and affluence.

Rajan exclaimed that he is their classmate Kastubh.

To which Ranjan replies " It's Kaustubh! But Why does this fella looks like 'Richie Rich'? "

The trio was amazed to see their classmate. And was interested in listening to his rags to riches story.

Kaustubh asks them how they were doing. In the little reunion, the trio discloses their plan to launch a startup. They ask him about his work life. Kaustubh reveals that he is the founder of the WhoopShoop website that shares viral content on the internet. Vicky asks him how did he start his endeavour and where did he get his funding from. Kaustubh replies that he started writing articles just for fun and people started liking it, his blogs became viral and the funds started pouring in.

Rajan asks him for the recipe of viral content.

Kaustub reveals that it's not "rocket science".

Usually, emotional, humorous videos, Pranks, or dangerous videos gets viral. And then he bids them goodbye.

Rajan is inspired by him and confesses that he wants to do something similar to this because it begets easy money and fame. Sahil restated that he is not interested in their lunacy. He will pave his own way. And asks them to leave him alone. Rajan tries to cajole him by telling him that they can meet his uncle to talk about a bank loan for his start-up.

They went to the bank and met Mr Chaddha. Whilst they were discussing about the loan, they were interrupted by a commotion.

Five men with guns & bags, break all CCTV's, and the emergency bell, to attempt a robbery.

One of the guys comes inside the manager's cabin, & points the gun at the bank manager, and starts threatening everyone to follow their instructions.

Rajan silently takes out his phone and records the entire incident. Sahil & Vicky are completely shocked and scared and didn't know what to do. All the robbers are continuously shouting. An army officer in civil dress observes that the robbers are very immature and they didn't even know how to properly hold a gun . The robbers took the money and tried to run away. One of them is caught by the army man. The other goons ran away fearing being caught. The complete incident is shot by Ranjan on his mobile phone. Later at night, he uploads that video on YouTube.

Ranjan wakes up with a call from a news channel requesting the real footage of the bank robbery. They were willing to pay for it. His video has gone viral on YouTube. He goes to Sahil and Vicky.

He wakes them up and explains to them that the robbery video that he has uploaded through Sahil's YouTube account, has gone viral. Sahil gets shocked and angry. He rebukes Ranjan for using his personal account for his amusement. He fears that if anything goes wrong he would be held accountable.

He receives a call from YouTube congratulating him that his account has been monetised asking him to add a sense account to start receiving money.

Everyone in college praises Sahil, Ranjan and Vicky for their valiant action in making that video which helped the police to catch the robbers.

Vicky & Ranjan wait for Sahil to convince him to make viral videos. They ask him to check the views of the Robbery video. He was amazed to see 1 million views on their first video!

Eventually, Sahil agrees to be their partner in making viral videos. However, he has his own terms & conditions. They decided to make some prank videos.

Finally, they recorded and posted their first prank video. They received amazing responses from people. They renamed the YouTube channel to 'Viral bhasad tv', which was formerly Sahil's account.

They started getting phone calls from their batch mates congratulating them for the viral videos.

They received more than 1 lakh views within a few hours.

With incredible response to the videos they celebrated and established their setup at Sahil's flat. They planned to recruit a new professional team member who could handle the camera and editing.

After interviewing 3-4 people. The trio had to settle with hiring Ehsan who used to work for a news channel. Because he was the only one who was available in their budget. Though this man throws many tantrums!

Bored with the monotony of the usual pranks the team decides to execute a horror prank.

According to the plan, Rajan would scare people away in a

witch costume. And Ehsan would record it. Ranjan started acting like an old hag.

The scared people started screaming and running in the opposite direction. After recording their scary reactions they confessed the victims of the prank that it's a YouTube prank.

They saw a well dressed man named Sunda coming out from a black Scorpio. He stops at a random wall & starts taking a leak. Vicky gives the action call to Ranjan, who starts moving towards this man. He got so frightened that he 'jumped out of his skin'!

Sunda started running and shouting, leaving behind everything. Ranjan follows him a little bit then comes back. Sahil & Vicky try to follow Sunda to reveal the prank but Sunda didn't stop.

They thought that they should apologise. They saw his car nearby and ran towards it. The front door was open and all of them were startled to see guns inside. They saw someone sleeping in the car. They are petrified to realise that the sleeping person is dead!

They ran towards their vehicles and fled the scene.

Two days later the team meets at Humayun's Tomb. Sahil and Ehsaan are disturbed by the incident. Ranjan & Vicky try to convince them that it was just an accident. They persuade them to continue making viral videos. Ranjan invites them to his relative's wedding.

The next day Ranjan and Ehsaan arrive at Sahil's place to pick him up. They create a scene by honking continuously while waiting for their friends. Annoyed, Sahil and Vicky get in the car which starts after throwing a few blow-ups. Finally, they reached the wedding venue.

Ranjan prompted everyone to dance in baraat and enjoy. During dinner, they observed a familiar face approaching them. They recognised it was Mr Srivastava.

He smiled and said, "Hello guys, remember you came to my office for a start-up idea." Sahil nodded his head. Mr Srivastava continued to say "Actually I thought about your project later on... It has potential but we need to work on some points. One of my assistants will coordinate with you! By the way, I haven't seen you in any other function. Are you from the Grooms side? "

Vicky answered confidently that its Rajan Arora's cousin's wedding. To this, Mr Srivastava retorted that it's Bhargav's & Shrivastav's function. It's his daughter's wedding and he gestured that they have crashed his daughter's wedding.

On asking the name of the groom from Ranjan, they realised that they had erroneously arrived at a wrong wedding.

All of them came out from the garden in a rush, continuously shouting at the inebriated weirdos

Ranjan & Ehsaan for their negligence. Being accused of crashing a wedding.

While everyone was arguing animatedly, someone puts a black cloth on their faces. Everyone started shouting in panic. They apologised for crashing the wedding and offered to pay the double amount for the food they had consumed. And promised to never repeat this offence.

They are abducted in a car and beaten up the entire night by some random goons.

The next day Vicky, Sahil and Ranjan find themselves in a big farmhouse. They saw a middle-aged, well-built man Ramakant Choudhary surrounded by ten bodyguards. Ranjan, Sahil and Vicky are battered by the goons. They heard a noise of a crying animal. They later realised, it was Ehsan's groaning voice while being beaten up by the goons. Suddenly four guys throws wickedly whacked Ehsaan on the floor. Ranjan, Vicky and Sahil are petrified and shocked.

Chaudhry calls Sunda and they recognised him, he was the same guy from the horror prank day. Chaudhary asks them what happened on that day. Sahil narrates the entire story. Then it is revealed that while running away Sunda left a bag containing some important documents on the way. And it is missing. Chaudhary asks them to fetch it otherwise he will kill them. He tells them that the bag contains money, IPhone and a Cd. They can keep the money and IPhone as a gift . He roared "Bring the CD or be ready to dig your own graves". He asks them to leave and sends four goons along with them.

Sunda is a hot-headed goon eager to kill at first sight. Sonu has some sympathy for the boys. (because he is an aspiring singer and anticipates that one day they might help him with his music video.) While the other two goons were just malevolent. They were the minions following the instructions.

The quest to find the Cd unravels a series of incidents that are unnerving yet amusing.

The politician's goons keep an eye on them following them all the time which scared them out of their wits. They argue with each other while finding the clue.

Finally, they trace their way back to the place 'where it all started' the venue of the prank which landed them in the trouble in the first place. They exhibit their detective skills and find the baba/ vagabond who was present that day. On enquiring, the vagabond confesses that he took the bag. He took the money and went to a shop to sell the laptop and iPhone but had to flee because of fear of the Police. To their dismay, He forgot the shop because of his drunken state.

Finally, they are able to locate the shop, Savita store. They reached a computer shop but couldn't find the CD, the shop owner mentions on a gun point that they do windows installations and provide their services for clients, he gives the name of the guys and a list of the places he went to provide the service that particular day and might have left it.

They explained their predicament to Ramesh Ji, the owner of the shop who shares four possible locations of the Cd and their addresses which were: Corporate office, lalwanihospital, Xavier's school and Ngo of Gb road respectively.

Chaudhry calls the team to inquire about the status. Sonu informs that an old man stole the bag. He took the money and tried to sell the iPhone to an electronic shop. And now the Cd is missing.

Chaudhry asks WWho played Chudail's/witch's role in the infamous prank?"

Ranjan puffed with pride replies humbly "Sir, actually, I am a great actor, so I got the opportunity to perform this prestigious role. "

Chaudhary asks his goons to break his four fingers. Sunda proceeds to follow the orders. Everyone shouts to save Ranjan but their efforts were futile. They couldn't save him.

Chaudhary asks Sonu to make video of their reactions while breaking them piece by piece if they dare to be over smart.

Ranjan loses his four fingers because of his jest.

They plan to visit the places where they could possibly find that Cd. Each location wreaths a new havoc. They cannot fathom how screwed they are (going to be)!

Sahil always bickers about his companions. And how he has landed in trouble because of them.

To their dismay the first location turns out to be Srivastava's office. They scheme a plan to get inside. Fearing they might be denied entry, thanks to their pathetic condition! Sahil explains their situation to Srivastava and begs for help. Even after getting access to the technical department he couldn't get his hands on the Cd and has to face a lot of embarrassment.

To get inside St. Xavier's school they hatch another plot - 'infiltrate the rock band'.

Ranjan and Ehsaan tries to manage the crowd by their musical dexterities and failed utterly meanwhile Vicky and Sahil try to find the Cd. They managed to find a Cd.

Sahil goes outside to call Sunda while looking out for Ranjan and Ehsaan. (Who managed to make a fool out of themselves! Followed by guards running aggressively behind them to throw them outside the campus.)

Sonu checks the Cd while speaking to Chaudhary.

He inquires " Who got the Cd."

 Vicky replies sheepishly " I found it! It's me who got it! "

Alas, the Cd turns out to be the wrong one!

Sonu asks Tabaro to break Vicky's hand!

Vicky says "WTF dude! You have already battered us! "

Sonu says " It's an order from high command. It's hardly a matter of two days then you can kiss your death! "

The boys are anxious and scared thinking about the worst possible things that could happen to them.

Third location turns out to be a red light area -GB road. All of them prepare themselves to enter the risky area.

Ehsaan somehow finds the guy who helped him during his news agency days. That guy accompanies them as a reporter. Ehsaan & Ranjan screw up themselves again! (by asking inappropriate questions.)

Vicky and Sahil reach NGO office where they meet Kishan ji who entirely misunderstands them and the the conversation takes another turn.

They did find a Cd. But they learned that it was the wrong one! Disappointed, they had to leave empty-handed.

They hear vociferous women coming towards them.

A crowd of women running behind miserable Ehsaan and Ranjan! Vicky and Sahil had to flee. They jumped into a car and took their friends along.

They rushed to the next location i.e. Lalwani hospital.

Sonu advises them to wait outside the hospital and spend the night in a car.

Rajan says " Bro, I am so hungry please get me a pizza before I Die".

Sonu: " Okay, I'll send it. Anything else? "

Rajan: "Mutton biryani, French fries, Chicken Burger, diet coke and Rasmalai for dessert. That's it! "

Sonu asks him if he has arrived at his father's wedding and asks him to shut up and sleep!

The next day they conspire to go inside the hospital.

Sahil acts like an injured patient. Ranjan, Vicky and Ehsaan act like his relatives.

Vicky and Ranjan go to find the whereabouts of Cd. While Ehsan was mockingly playing with some surgical equipment, Sahil is taken to the ICU.

Vicky and Ranjan are desperate to find out the Cd. They are shown all the boxes. To their misfortune,

the original Cd was nowhere to be found. Ranjan takes out a random Cd stealthily. They came out to see Sahil and Ehsaan running away followed by a group of people.

They get a call from Sunda and are ordered to steer towards Humayun's tomb.

Sunda "We have got orders to kill one of them. "

Sonu " But they have time till evening"

Sunda " They didn't get the Cd. If we kill one of them, then it might work."

They grabbed Sahil and started hitting him. Sahil is bent down on his knees crying and shouting. One of the goons pointed a gun towards his head.

Suddenly Ranjan hands over a Cd and pleads them to leave Sahil.

Vickey : "You ducking preposterous moron! You had the Cd all along and you didn't even bother to tell us! You are going to get us killed!

Ranjan : "This is a random Cd that i took from the hospital. They were going to kill him I had to do something! "

Sunda :" I knew he had it all along! "

Ranjan : 'Sir please leave them alone, it's all my gaffe/blunder. Please check the Cd.

Sonu asks to check the Cd.

Vicky: "You ignoramus nincompoop! Now we are definitely going to die! They'll check it and it has nothing! "

Ranjan: "Don't worry. Sir, I have a request. Please let them go we still have time till evening. I will stay with you. You can do anything to me. Please let them go. We didn't get the opportunity to check if this Cd is the correct one. Please give us the last chance to find the Cd just in case it is not the one you were looking for."

Sunda instructs other goons to check the Cd and asks them to thrash the quartet if it turns out to be the wrong one.

Their Cd player didn't work so they couldn't check the Cd.

Sunda shoots Ranjan on the leg and asks them to be prepared to dig their own graves if they fail to find the Cd within four hours.

Everyone leaves for Savita computers & sales.

They look at the CCTV footage of the two days after Baba's arrival. At some point they saw two kids around 12 to 13, one of them is sitting on the owners chair who happens to be the owner's son . Having fun playing games with his friend and saw his friend taking a Cd.

They get the kid's address which happens to be Shivani's house. The door is opened by Shivani's mother. They were in such a pathetic condition, she thought they are some random beggars. Then Sahil reveals everything in brief. And enquires about the Cd.

Vikas, Shivani's brother reveals that the Cd is with his sister and she is at the college fest . After calling her he discovers that the cd is with Sandy who is at the open theatre preparing for the ramp show and dance competition .

Sahil calls his parents and tells them that he has dropped the idea of the start-up and would get a job . He gets emotional, tells his parents to take care and tears rolled down his cheeks.

Sahil is thoroughly aware that he is in grave danger. One more mistake and they might be as dead as a dodo!

Sonu shows them the time, they only have 10 minutes left to save themselves. If they do not reach on time with the correct Cd, they will shoot Vicky and Ranjan. They took both of them out of the Scorpio at gunpoint.

Sahil meets Shivani who asks him if he is okay and inquiries about his pathetic condition. Sahil apologised for everything. He confides that he is in huge trouble and is unsure if he could ever meet her again. He asks her to give his wallet to his parents. He told her that he wished to propose to marry her. He confesses his love to her and requests her to take care.

Shivani is scared and starts following him.

Sahil takes the Cd from Sandy. He is anxious because only five minutes are left to save their lives.

This time Chaudhary's goons will not spare their lives. He frantically checks the Cd on the laptop. He is shocked to see a massive money scandal committed by the same politician (Choudhary) . This CD was proof that could implicate him.

Their time is almost over and Sahil runs towards the back gate of the college. He hears 2-3 gunshots. He saw Ehsaan crying bitterly and realizes that Ranjan and Vicky were absent. Filled with remorse and guilt he stood aghast at the sight and falls on his knees devastated. The memories of his dearest friends started playing in his mind. He started groaning in pain. He couldn't stop his tears.

Everyone on the other side of the road saw the Cd in his hand.

Suddenly he heard the noise of crackers. He realised a celebratory wedding procession/ Baarat coming towards him. Then he saw Vicky and Ranjan coming from the backside of the car after peeing asking Sonu where to wash their hands. Sahil suddenly realises that he had misunderstood the scenario. At the same time, a random guy mistook him as a beggar, offered him ten rupees and suggested him to die somewhere else and leave this path for the Barat.

Vicky and Ranjan glanced at Sahil in shock!

VICKY yells at him to bring the Cd quickly before they get shot by the goons.

Ranjan "I think he is performing prayer or voodoo maybe! Bhai he's lost his mind! Please throw a shoe at his face. He has got the Cd and yells at Sahil to come soon.

SAHIL crosses the road and hugs his friends with joy.

Sonu takes the Cd and gets it assessed. They called Chaudhary to inform him that they have found the original Cd. Chaudhary advises the Boys to forget about this incident.

Sahil and Ehsaan ran towards their car, Vicky grabs Ranjan forcing him in the car. All of them flee the scene.

The next morning Chaudhary was greeted by cops while he was sleeping on his khaat. He gets arrested.

"Your scandal has gone viral" exclaims the policeman

After 4 days Sahil, Ranjan, Vicky and Ehsaan curiously ask

Sahil how did Choudhari's video go viral

Sahil reveals that when he saw the video of a politician accepting bribes associated with a big scam. He could not accept such audacious plundering of India's wealth. So he went on to uncover/expose the corrupt politician of the country. He uploaded the video on YouTube from a fake account and deleted the video as soon as it got posted by other accounts and became viral.

The truth is that whatever one seeks to hide and cover up eventually works its way up to the light and becomes known!

Sahil turns the tables on Chaudhary. The video is leaked online and a big secret is revealed which exposes the politician which leads to criminal investigations.

Corruption remains to be the largest limitation to a country's progress. But there is a new generation finding creative, ingenious unified ways to fight against it.

Present day:

We never imagined that this will reach to this massive stage when we started on, but to my knowledge a lot of things just happens without us knowing, 'chahe kitni baketi karo life ki bhasad kabhi khatam nhi hoti'

GRANDPARENTS

It was close to the Diwali season and I was just cleaning up the bookshelves this morning, just as any regular day, overhearing dadu and daadi talk about some old memories and going through some old pictures, happy and full of nostalgic conversations, I immediately opened up my phone to hit the record button keeping it near them, Daadi, 'You remember the time when he filled his pocket with firecrackers',

Dadu, ' yes, how can I forget I saved him otherwise he would have burned himself badly'

Just then their phone rang and it was their grandson, who they love a lot, picking up the phone aunty talks and asking about his plan to come visit them this diwali, but he refuses by saying he is overloaded with work and won't be able to get holidays, filled up either sadness aunty keeps the phone when dadu calls on to me telling me to make an Indian sweet dish (keer) tonight with an extra sweet and dry fruits.

I could see the pain and sadness in their eyes, it occurred to me to send their recorded voice mail to bhaiya, hoping if it could change anything.

The next following day, morning the door bell rang when I opened the door, there was bhaiya, playing the voice mail I send him, remembering and being grateful towards dadu, a big smile came to aunty's face and dadu as they were talking about all the memories together.

The happiness I saw in both of their faces made me smile and content, at that very moment bhaiya looked at me and said so much without even saying anything.

Celebrating the festival together in an Indian culture is the power of relations and sharing this happiness together is what makes people unique and kind.

FITRAT

"Where are you going Arjun? And whose car is this?" Ram shouted with warmth and concern.

Arjun pretends to not have heard and walks away abruptly and leaves in his car. Arjun Gautam was born to a lower middle-class family in Meerut as the son of a police constable, Ram Manohar. Unlike his father, Arjun never believed in working hard or being truthful. All he aspired was to become rich, though not bothered about the path he takes. Throughout his adulthood he had found one or the other short cut for quick money and he was proud of him. His father contrast to this, despite having enough opportunities for taking bribe and getting rich like many of his colleagues never took a penny that wasn't earned by his sweat and toil. He hated the ideologies of his son and prayed earnestly for him to leave the grey life and find a stable job. And during Arjun's college days, every morning they argued and fought and it was after constant pressure, Arjun completed his graduation. And now, when his father comes in the morning to have any conversation, he walks away without talking. And it became a routine in their life. But the father was always proud of the intelligence of his child and wished with all his heart that he used it in the right ways.

One morning when rain was pouring down the roof of their home, Ram Manohar receives a call from his senior,

"Ram ji, namaste. Your son is arrested by the new CI. He was driving a stolen car that too without license. Please come soon."

Ram without even wearing a raincoat took his bike and rushed to the station. Just like he feared, his son was arrested. Ram went and saw that his son was sitting in the old wooden bench head hung low. He placed his hands-on Arjun's shoulder and pressed as if giving him assurance of protection and rushed to the CI's office. Ram begged the CI to leave him out without any charges in word of keeping him away from all mischiefs and crimes in future. Arjun who sat outside was noticing the number of politicians and businessmen who came in between with money to offer bribe. He saw them all going inside the room which had a nameplate *Anirudh Prasad I P S*. That immediate moment, Arjun realized the profit he could earn and the power would come along with being an officer. Thinking about all this, his father came back from CI's office.

"Beta, go home. I've taken care of this. Please I beg of you. Don't put me in such a position again. In my entire career I have not held my head low. And now because of you I had to stoop down without any self-respect."

Arjun left again without saying anything and while walking to home, he called a friend of his from college who was in Delhi. Through him he collected all the details he wanted about the UPSC exam and without saying goodbye to his parents, with all the money he had, took train to Delhi. He reached Delhi the

next evening and took admission in a coaching center and took a
room nearby which he shared with Balraj Sahni an aspiring civil
service officer. Balraj was attempting it for the second time and
was putting in more and more efforts to crack the exam somehow.
He was glad now he could prepare along with someone and the
two become good friends. But gradually Arjun realized that he
cannot put in all the efforts needed for the preparation and he was
about to give up when he read the newspaper report about the scam
in state PCS exam. Arjun who already had enough connections
through which he could collect all the information, did that. He
understood it was comparatively easier and with all the information
he collected, good and bad, prepared for it. He also managed to get
a fraud backward certificate in order to get reservation and passed
the exam with a lower rank. He became a Block Development
Officer nearby his home purposefully not because he wanted to
meet his family often, but because he knew the land mafia was
heavily active and he could profit from it. While he was doing
his graduation, he saw how Madhav Singh, their MLA and other
government officials, top to bottom, made huge amount of money
illegally through land mafia. Arjun always kept that in mind and
from the day he joined, he started helping the mafia and goons
and built his political connections for his personal gains. And the
toxic symbiotic relation between them spread like virus. Arjun's
greed increased day by day and within a short span, he built his
own home and brought a luxury car. His father but still held on to
his ideologies and never once came to the home built with dowry.
He lived the ordinary life which he earned through his blood and
sweat. Arjun even started exploiting the poor ones by grabbing their
lands illegally and helped Madhav Singh to own more land. And

because of the widespread mis' happenings, gradually the national media started covering the news and soon the central government posted a young brave IPS officer as the new ACP. It was none other than, Balraj Sahani. And as soon as he joined, he marked his arrival with arresting the local goons who threatened the poor ones and forcefully took away their money. Arjun was intimidated by the news because he knew the dedication of Balraj and nothing materialistic can bribe him. Arjun by the time had already gained strong political connections and kept a clean track record with his cunningness. But Balraj knew Arjun's hands weren't clean; he was financially more stable than an IPS officer like himself that too in short span of time. And that's when Balraj remembered an early conversation he had with Arjun about his father who was a police constable. Balraj dig more about him and came to know that Ram Manohar was an honest cop and called him to his office.

"So, you don't have an answer to how your son gained all this money? Have you seen his house? His car? Answer me Ram ji" Balraj tried to ask sternly for getting some answers.

"I don't know sir."

And Balraj did not ask more because he knew, Ram did not know much about his son. He said Ram could leave and while going back ram turned and said,

"Sir, if you could change him, I'd be the most thankful. I will help you however I could."

Balraj knew then, Arjun had done many mistakes and his entire life has been a short cut.

Arjun believed he was safe and continued to help Madhav and his family to gain more land and money though with more caution. While Arjun was faking a document for Madhav, his doorbell rang.

Arjun opened the door and was surprised to see his father in front of him. It has been almost two years since he built the home, and it was now his father came to see him. He welcomed him and Ram Manohar was shocked to see the extravagant life of his son.

"How are you son?"

"Look at me Papa. I haven't been better."

"I am scared Arjun."

Arjun gets irritated and goes to the kitchen to ask the maid to bring tea for his father. He comes to see that his father is standing outside the door wearing his chappals to go back.

"Papa."

"You are nothing but a pawn Arjun. They are using you."

"And I am using them."

"In my four-decade long career, I have seen only two endings for these stories. Either you die in some encounter, or the lords you serve will get rid of you themselves. You still have got time. Confess to Balraj sir. He is a nice officer. If you surrender, he will help you."

"Even I have seen the world papa. I can take care of myself. Please don't bother."

Ram turns back and leaves,

"Papa"

"Yes beta."

"You need some money?"

Ram like typical Arjun walked away pretending he didn't hear.

Few days passed and Madhav called Arjun to let him know about an illegal consignment that is coming the next day for which he wants the clearance. Arjun finds out who many are going to be posted and where the checking will be. Madhav's goons got all this information and also instruction by Arjun not to fire at any cost. The goons just scared the police force away and the consignment reached Madhav safely. After completing the work, the gang leader called Arjun to say thank you.

"Arjun bhai, work is done. Thank you. And that Balraj won't live longer. Remember him arresting that Anwar's gang when he came? Today they attacked him and one police officer also died saving him."

"Oh really?! Where did it happen?"

"Here nearby somewhere."

"Who died?"

"Some Ram Manohar. Just a constable."

Arjun dropped the phone down and sank to the chair nearby. He was shattered to hear the death of his father by the same men with whom he does trade. He cried and mourned for his father. Arjun returned to his ancestral home leaving everything he made illegally behind. Soon after that Arjun determined to destroy Madhav, starts to plot against him. Arjun dig every inside information about the illegal things he and his family was planning to do and feeds it to the police. Meanwhile, Balraj too, moved by the sacrifice made my Ram to save his life, pledges to make Arjun come before justice. And it did not take Balraj much time to realize all the illegal activities Arjun was engaged in. He even found out that Arjun's backward certificate was fake. Balraj documented all the evidences against Arjun and was moving the legal formalities to go against him.

Arjun was consumed by guilt, for stealing money from innocent labors, for taking the land of the poor, for mistreating his father and many more. He was adamant to destroy Madhav very soon and in the hurry, he left many loopholes. Madhav soon found out the informer was none other than Arjun.

Finally, Balraj issued the arrest warrant and went to Arjun's home and found out from his maid that Madhav came and took him. Balraj with all his power, tracked him down and went to arrest him. He reached the forest nearby where he himself was attacked few months back. And there he saw Arjun tied to a tree almost beaten to death. It was the same place Ram lost his life and the last moments of the poor soul came to his mind.

"sir, please help him. He is good at heart. Please save my son."
"I will Ram ji."
And then Ram Manohar rested in peace.

Arjun almost unconscious losing blood still held his head high and smiled like his father. Balraj then saw Madhav aiming a gun at Arjun from a distance. And then all the birds chirped and flew away hearing the gun shots. Arjun fainted.

Balraj had shooted madhav and his goons and rushed to the hospital with injured Arjun. His life was saved but Balraj made sure justice was served. Arjun was imprisoned for 8 years for conspiracy and fraud. But fate was kind to him. With the help of Balraj and also because of his good behavior during imprisonment, he came out within 6 years. And while he got out, he received his belongings in which he touched the most priceless thing he ever possessed. The bravery medal of his father which was awarded posthumously. None of his relatives went to receive the medal because Arjun was in prison and his mother too died alone during his prison life. He came out to see that his house was completely destroyed by Madhav's gang.

Arjun devastated left his hometown to a nearby city and started working as a daily wage laborer in a sweet shop. No one knew who he was or what his name was. It was his second life and he himself gave him a new name too. He still uses his smart ways, but now it is to help the poor and needy. Gradually through constant hard work he pulls his life back. Time passed and he is 32 years old now. And it was his father's tenth death anniversary. He finally decided to go back. He went back to his home town and goes to the place where his father died and where he almost died and was reborn. He sat there and mourned for his father and suddenly felt a hand on his shoulder and turned back;

"Where have you been Arjun?".

It was Balraj. Balraj tried to track down Arjun but couldn't because of the low key life he led. Balraj is now working with UP ATS and had come a long way in his career.

"You have suffered enough Arjun. Move on. At least for your father's sake. Your father died on duty and you could get his job. I will help you. It's is enough of vanvaas for you. Go home."

"Sir, I can prepare for PCS working in force, right?"

"Of course, you can. And you should. All your charged are clear now. Go for it Arjun."

They walked back with peace filled heart to a different life.

CAN WE SHARE?

Overwhelming first day of a corporate world can be exciting as well as full of adjustment. Here our karthik knowing and getting information by his boss Rahul bajaj, as he goes around introducing the departments in an IT office where he is going to start his first job. Looking around he notices a girl sitting at her desk working, goes in his office to sit and chat at little when Boss calls Ramu and tells him to bring water for kartik and call Bhanu inside, Bhanu the most accommodating employee. Boss introduces Bhanu and kartik, just when bhanu, steps up to get shake hand, kartik immediately gets up to take the glass of water from Ramu the security of the company but almost all the menial jobs for the company.

A little awkward moment for Bhanu but there soon after he tells Bhanu to show kartik his desk and the rest of the office essentials, leaving Rahul's office Bhanu continues to introduce kartik to the group briefly and just casually drinking his tea goes to his own cabin. The first few seconds for kartik to sit in his chair and to adjust to the surrounding there is a curiosity with a bit nervousness, noticing this girl sitting in a yellow dress and working diligently without getting distracted, who after a while notices kartik and gives him a nice glance as to see who is new colleagues.

Beginning the next day, kartik enters with a fresh smile and excitement, greeting Ramu but instead Ramu reverts with a gritty comment for not coming on time. Kartik handles it well with a smile and moves to his desk, just after noticing the girl again, he starts working when bhanu comes in with a few files and tells kartik to finish and hand it over to him after lunch.

Kartik gets up to get himself a glass of water and because not being attentive spills it over and walks over to his desk, when bhanu from behind spills over and commands Ramu to clean up but Ramu reacts to bhanu saying he takes care of the security not the basic chores, bhanu says he'll tell this to his the boss, when soon after Ramu cleans up the area acting as a boss himself.

It's the lunch time, and as everyone leaves their desks, kartik tries to communicate to the girls, thinking of having lunch with them when bhanu interrupts saying to have lunch with him in his cabin with him. Kartik unable to refuse because of a fresher walks away with bhanu, kartik trying to make contact with this girl, unable to get a reach, lurking over the next day while filling up the coffee cup, one for her, it seems as the luck of poor kartik runs out everytime this time bhanu comes and taps kartik at his back spilling the coffee kartik is holding in his shirt and the floor, having an argument they part ways when their boss walks up having a conversation with someone over phone, almost about to slip cursing the situation asking who did such a thing be calls on to ramu, while ramu seems to be enjoying a song with his earphones on, unable to listen to his boss, Rahul starts yelling at ramu, when his attention comes back to the situation for a second he was unable to mute his phone, then coming over to see what happened he is confused over who did it when their boss asked them what is happening these days with these pills banu and ramu argue with each other soon his boss and bhanu commands ramu to clean up the mess buy new andremo again get to each other after their boss leaves and bhanu with a little agitation tells ramu to do his job with a sarcastic gesture ramu does every time. karthik cleans up and comes out of the washroom when Ramu enters in and they have a conversation Ramu, 'so you are the one spilling coffee and water lately'. Kartik, ' No, it's not me, why would I ever spill coffee on myself, it was bhanu.' At the same time Kartik asks ramu about the girl he is been wanting to talk to whose name is Rumi and is from Chandigarh ramu confirmed. Having a glance at rumi over the file the other day Kartik got frightened when ramu taps him on his shoulders to give a file send by his boss to correct and give it to Rumi ma'am his excitement knew no limits and he started working just when bhanu came to take the same file and they fight over the file, with much authority bhanu takes the file with him leaving Kartik speechless and annoyed.

A noise soon after of a file being slammed comes from Rahul's office, Rumi and Rahul having an argument over an project idea, from which their boss is not satisfied even through rumi has researched and prepared it for the 4th time, Rahul with an arrogant attitude tells rumi to change and bring it again, soon after this heated argument rumi walks out the cabin and out to get some fresh air, kartik not missing such an opportunity this time goes out, pretending to talk on the phone with some official person about his house showing some kind of tensed situation over the phone, after which he fills up a cup of coffee and walks near Rumi, Rumi notices and starts a conversation with kartik overhearing his talk on phone asks about, why he sounded tensed, kartik reasons it as some financial issue he is going through. Kartik asks rumi for a cup of coffee but she refuses saying, he can share if something is bothering him, kartik turning the attention and asks about Rumi and how she is seem more upset over something.

Rumi, ' I don't know, it's like everytime this happens, one project he is never satisfied makes correction, and tells me to change, what should I do then'. Kartik then insists on getting a coffee for her but rumi refuses, looks at kartik and insists on sharing from the same cup. They continue to chat over this cup of coffee. Rumi asks kartik about what happened and he continues to lie about the scenario over the phone as, municipal party thinks his house is on their property and he just have renewed the house, taken a loan and his father is a heart patient. Rumi with a concerned voice saying to kartik that hoe difficult it must be for him. Rumi tells about her plan when asked by kartik as she has to do the same old job as her house is not here so she could go and relax for somedays. Rumi, 'where are you from? ' kartik, ' Delhi only so I could go back to my house. 'Actually we met before, I tired to talk to you, honestly my heart races everytime u tired to, I spilled coffee and water twice because of it. 'Well, how many people are in your house?

Rumi, 'mom, dad and a younger brother who is also an engineer, dad is a professor and mom homemaker'what about you?

Kartik without thinking starts to inform about his family ' dad, mom, sister who got married, my dad owns a business, I just finished my engineering so he told me to join and work as this is his friends office, and to learn professional and coporative skills, with a very casual demeanor he went on while rumi looks at him with a blank look and seriously listening to him, at the same time kartik remember the lie is made to start a conversation with rumi starts to stammer and tryimg to explain his act, after a few minutes of silence she looks at him and bursts into laughter, both of them started laughing at the situation and shared a cup of coffee.

SHATRANJ

'Shatranj' is a story about Love, friendship, Passion, Politics, Betrayal, Existence and Revenge happening in the chessboard of Delhi among the chess pieces Gogi, Bawana, Kartik, Kishan and Ashwath.

Gogi was born in Delhi. He always wanted to win and do big in life. He was a very ambitious boy. He was interested in sports and had a never say die attitude even towards smallest of school football games to local cricket matches. His winning spirit would sometimes go beyond the game so much so that it would turn into aggression and he would end up fighting if someone cheats during the match. This made Gogi, a popular among his friends very early in life, One of those friends was Ashwath.

Ashwath Sharma was a very bright student since childhood. Being a Lecturer's Son, he never had difficulties in studies, mostly in maths, which was Gogi's major study concern. Ashwath used to like cricket, but whenever his batting turn would come, other players used to bully him asking him to purposely go for hit wicket and hit the bat to the stumps. One day, when Ashwath went for Hit-wicket on being bullied by players, a guy didn't like this and opposed it blatantly calling this as pure cheating and fought for Ashwath. Never in his life had ashwath saw any friend taking stand for him, Infact Ashwath hardly had any friends in school. Ashwath kept batting then and played a very good innings though they lost the match. When the match got finished, ashwath went to the boy who stood for him to thank him. " Mujhe Cheating Pasand nahi bhai. Teri Jagah koi aur bhi hota to jhagda kar leta. Aisa hi hoon main. ", said the boy.

Ashwath shook his hand and said " Thank you bhaiya !"

" Abey bhaiya waiya mat bol. Gogi naam hai mera. Aur Kal se open kara kar. "

Ashwath found a new brother like friend in Gogi. Infact, Gogi was the only friend ashwath could make. Being in the same school where his father used to teach, ashwath never got fair credit for his talent and was always envied and targetted for favourism, as all school teachers used to go soft on him and hard on other students. So ashwath used to only concentrate on studies and all the friends he could have had, he only found it in one guy, 'Gogi'.

Gogi was not just a fierce, strong and aggressive bad boy, there was another side of Gogi which no one knew, which was a soft, sensitive and caring being, which only surekha had an idea of.

Surekha was the only daughter of a High Court Judge Mr. Purshottam Gupta. Being an only child, she was always pampered but kept under very protective layer by her family. Guptas used to have social gatherings at their home, of which Gogi's family was a regular guest. Gogi used to feel good that his family, especially his grandfather, Veer Pratap Ji enjoys a special place everywhere. Veer Pratap though an old Man, his calibre and high power can be traced from the fact that, He is respected and treated as a father figure " Veer Ji ", and the summons like, " Veer Ji ne Kaha hai..." does all the work in and around Delhi. No one had the power or courage to say No to him. All one has to say is , " Veer Ji ne Kaha hai..." And it has an authority of a higher order which no one used to question or dare not to follow. Gogi, as a boy, used to observe this keenly.

Surekha also being a Judge's daughter was also surrounded by an ambience of power but she hardly had any interest in this. She wanted to explore the world and see that Delhi which she was kept aloof of. In one of the social gatherings, she saw a boy smoking cigarette secretly at the backyard of their house. She went near him and start scolding him and threatened to tell her father. She agreed to keep this a secret on a condition that the boy will teach her how to smoke the cigarette. She takes one drag and coughes heavily. The boy laughs and she tells him that this is her first and last cigarette. The boy smiles and tells her that she made a good decision and that smoking is anyway injurious to health. She gets confused and asks him why does he smoke then ? " Aisa hi hoon main... " , Says Gogi and starts coughing heavily. Surekha couldn't start laughing and seeing this goofup, Gogi too joins in her laughter.

After this, at any social gathering, whenever Surekha used to find Gogi, she would hang around with him, eat dinner together, hang around in social functions and surekha used to talk about everything she desired, which she couldn't do at her home with anyone. She finds a very special friend in Gogi. With time, Gogi would meet Surekha outside their house. Gogi started bunking his Maths Tution classes and surekha would lie about going at her friend's place to study to spend time with Gogi. Gogi would take surekha on long drive on his Yamaha RX-100 bike and took her to all places wherever surekha desired. One day Surekha wished to see a movie in a Multiplex which had all the abuse and foul language. Gogi didn't agree on this and first time surekha and gogi fights on this. Surekha doesn't talk with gogi for a week then.Gogi finally agrees and they go for a movie. While watching the movie, some rowdy men pass foul comments on Surekha and Gogi loses him temper. He starts shouting at them and soon it turns out into a big fight. Soon other people in the cinema stops the brawl and Gogi takes Surekha with him and drops her at her home. In the whole journey he doesn't utter a work. Surekha says thank you to Gogi. She didn't know that she is so important for anyone that one can literally fight for her and gives gogi a hug which is not a normal hug. Gogi kisses her forehead and says , " I can fight against the world for you. I will always be there for you ! " Surekha has tears in her eyes and smile on her face. She leaves saying good bye. Gogi feels something he never had and leaves for his home with this special feeling on his bike.

As the time passes, Gogi's interest for studies go less. He spends most of his time riding bike with surekha and rest of the time he spends is in his newly found interest, boxing, after the brawl at movie theatre. He takes active interest in boxing which can vent his ambitious and raw spirit. Surekha even gifts Gogi a pair of red boxing glove and supports his ambition. Veer Ji doesn't like this. Veer Ji always tells Gogi's mother that she should not spoil him by letting him do whatever he wishes too. He should take studies seriously, go foreign for further study and give a different direction to their political party. Gogi finds it fruitless. He knows he is a successor to Veer Ji and after him he will be the next Veer Ji. What Gogi fails to see and what Gogi doesn't know is what amount of work Veer Ji have had done to achieve this powerful position. Veer Ji used to be Veer Pratap, an orphan boy who used to throw newspapers every morning cycling the whole area of old delhi. He then used to read all the news from major newspapers. He educated himself through it and by observing people showing them Delhi as a guide. Later, Veer Ji started his political journey as an independent candidate of an old delhi ward he used to throw newspapers in and ended up creating his own political party named " Jan Shakti ". His party did all the necessary developments which no ruling party ever bothered to care about and provided necessary help to all poor and needy sections of Delhi. Veer Ji's Party today plays an influential role in Delhi's Politics. No CM today can sit on chair if not being supported by Veer Ji's party as Veer Ji enjoys all the popular support and respect in Delhi.

Veer Ji wants to expand his power further and has a vision for his party and Delhi, he knows that Delhi politics now needs a Young Leader to steer it with new ideas and contemporary advance developments which is a must to progress. He doubts whether Gogi has this Vision . Veer Ji knows what education can do which mere hierarchy cannot as he himself has made a life out of reading just newspapers.

One Fine morning, when Veer Ji was reading newspaper with

a tea, Gogi tells Veer Ji that he wants to enroll in Delhi University College for B.A in Political Science but he didn't get enough grades to qualify for. Veer Ji gets amused by this fact. He feels a hint of responsibility Gogi is subconsciously trying to understand. Veer Ji assures Him not to worry and It will be done. Gogi touches Veer Ji's feet and leaves. While going, Veer Ji tells him to stop using bikes now as he is no more a boy and start using a car now. He further tells him, " Car me 2 nahi 5 log baith sakte hain. Iska matlab Chalane wale ko 5 guna jyada jyada zimmedari se gaadi chalani padti hai. " And hands him the keys.

Gogi goes to pick surekha from her house and surekha is amused to see Range Rover. When Surekha enquires about getting all excited, Gogi puts the shades on and says…" Veer ji ne kaha hai…" And they both start laughing. Gogi asks her where does she want to go today, surekha says there is hardly any place left for us to explore now, gogi says there is one favourite place which he likes to visit often. He keeps seeing surekha and moves ahead to kiss Surekha but surekha puts a hand over his lips and says I too and kisses on it. A horn starts blowing from behind and Gogi gets irritated for a romantic moment getting spoiled. Surekha laughs a bit and asks him to take her to 'long drive'. Gogi puts the shades on, starts the car and sets the car in motion showing a middle finger to the car behind his through his window.

We see another car entering into Delhi Campus. Inside which are sitting Ashwath and his Father who is now a Dean of Delhi University. Ashwath tells him that he didn't like this and he already has suffered a lot. He wants to create his own identity now and doesn't want to spend his graduation life under his name. He asks him to stop the car and tells him that it's not that he disrespects him as a father or as a lecturer. His father understands that and asks him if he needs anything he is there but he must stay away from people like Gogi in this campus and that it leads nowhere. Ashwath gets irritated by this and leaves.

Ashwath enters into campus and sits into his L.L.B classroom. First time in his life he feels he is a different guy. On being asked for his introduction he tells everything to the class teacher except for his father's name and his occupation. During the class, He asks many questions to the class teacher regarding justice and argues on importance of justice in today's modern world over importance of liberty as a significant thought to run the society and the world. Everyone gets impressed including the class teacher. As the class finishes, he sees a black range rover making its way into the campus. Ashwath gets in all awe of this car. The Car stops at a canteen nearby and a Guy and Girl comes out. The security guard asks him to keep the car out, ashwath sees that the guy gives him some money and the key and the guard takes the car to park himself in the parking lot. Everyone around the canteen and the campus, sees this and are surprised to see this. Suddenly a Guy comes in front of car and stops the watchman. He tells them that this is wrong and this is not justified. Rules are equal for everyone and no one can bend it with their money or muscle power. The guy says his name is Bawana, He is a student here in Campus and he hasn't seen this guy before. He Asks for his ID. " Veer Pratap Ji ka Pota, Gogi ! Yehi ID hai ". The guy takes his own ID card from his wallet and tells Gogi, " This is what ID means. And this is earned by taking enormous efforts, study, hard work and passion. My name is Bawana, Son of Shri Lakshman Rao, late MLA of ghaziabad constituency. But I don't use his name in public to show power and seek respect. " Gogi feels humiliated and angry at this. He is about to lose his temper but surekha comes in and says sorry. She explains that it's not him, it's her, she wanted to drive Range Rover and she couldn't resist entering canteen with a range rover and that Gogi was infact stopping her but it's her who had insisted. She takes the key from the guard in hurry and says she shouldn't have brought Gogi to her college. Gogi stops her and says that, " It's my college too. And about individuality if someone wants to know, an A4 size paper doesn't decide anyone's qualification and qualification doesn't decide one's character. " He gives a tough look to Bawana saying this. He Snatches key from Surekha's hand and leaves. On taking the car behind, people all around the canteen starts approaching bawana, for what he has done is a rare sight. They all start clapping to Bawana's act of courage. The canteen manager on seeing this sight says in sarcasm, " Mil gaya inko naya President."

Gogi boxes heavily in the evening session. He couldn't sleep over this identity remark thrown at him by bawana. Next day, He wakes up early in the morning and goes to college with his black range rover, this time parking it in the campus. He starts his B.A first class with all good intent to learn. He questions passionately about what is right and why actions are much important than talks and that diplomacy is pointless in politics. In the introduction class itself, He argues that what is rightfully yours is yours and there can be no diplomacy about it. The teacher starts giving examples of co-operation and how co-operation can only help in the end. Other students starts pointing out that as Gogi never really had to adjust in his life and all the things were only spoon fed to him, he will never understand what co-operation is. " He knows the spelling of cooperation, that's enough. " Everyone starts laughing at this comment including the professor. A boy in the last bench stands and says with a firm and clear voice that, " Sir, a system needs both cooperation for establishment and rebellion for change. Every order is being built upon by co-operation but with prolonged time, every order or system becomes stagnant and at such point, it becomes necessary for an external force, to breach diplomacy and take actions to do what is being rightfully needed to be done. Gogi was speaking about this action Sir. " Kartik then starts quoting Karl Marx and mythological reference of samudra manthan as thesis, anti-thesis and synthesis as a political thought. Gogi suddenly lifts his head and looks behind to see who is the guy. The class teacher aks his name, "Kartik" , the boy says. The teacher then asks his full name, kartik says nothing and he makes an eye contact with Gogi. Gogi sees something, the look which is familiar to him. The look which knows, a part of which he carries in his self but is hidden, a look of a fatherless child. The bell rings. The conversation remains incomplete and everyone goes out except Gogi and Kartik. Gogi says thanks to Kartik for what he has done has really touched him. He tells him that he doesn't need to feel bad about his full name. Or any past for that matter. And asks him where has he learnt such deep thoughts from? Kartik says he didn't go to any school, he had learnt everything from books. He used to read books in his orphanage home. His warden used to be very kind as she didn't have her own son and he was alone all his life except for books. Gogi tells him that from now on, he never has to feel that he is alone and he never has to depend upon anyone for studying or for anything in life again.

Karthik feels very soothing about this. That none has made this gesture to him. Thinking about this in a metro, he goes to a coffee shop at canaught place. We see ashwath is sitting in that coffee house with a girl. Ashwath explains to her something, gives her some books and tells her that if she needs to crack MBA its important she understands these topics well. And if she needs any help in this topic she doesn't need to ask Dean uncle, she can directly contact him. They both go to the counter to pay the bill, " Its 550 sir. 2 Capaccino and one club cheese grilled sandwich. " Ashwath pays the bill and they both leave. As they both go out of the cafe, they are stopped by the counter boy and hands over the mobile to the Girl. Ashwath feels good about this honesty, he takes his wallet out to give him some money to which the boy says, " Honesty is not something I am paid for sir, I am paid to serve you coffee, the bill of which you had already paid. Thank you sir, do visit again. " The girl asks his name. "Karthik !" The boy says. " Thank you Karthik. It's rare to see guys like you. I really mean it." Says Devyani. Karthik looks in her eyes and says thank you Mam. " it's Devyani, call me Devyani. " Karthik eyes shine in that moment. Ashwath bids bye and everyone leaves. Devyani turns back while leaving to see Karthik again but Karthik doesn't look back and everyone leaves.

Devyani is a very talented and grounded girl. She is the only daughter of Business Man, Gurmukh Gujral. She is good in dance, badminton and reads a lot. There is hardly anything that Devyani wants to learn and her father says no to. Gujral is a very progressive business Man and free Father. He raises Devyani not in a protective shell but an explorative environment. It is this free space which had made Devyani to Join her father's business not as her daughter but as an accomplished MBA graduate from IIM. Gujral and Ashwath's Father were good friends. Infact, Ashwath's father Had given money as a loan to Gujral on various occasions in his initial business set-up days which they usually make fun of often saying that , the interest has compounded and now he owes crores.

In a college canteen, we see Gogi hanging out with Surekha and Kartik. He asks for canteen manager and suddenly ashwath says the bill is on me. We ashwath coming in and joining him. He is happily shocked to see Gogi after so long. Ashwath sees surekha and asks Gogi if she is the same surekha he had told him once. Gogi turns awkward and introduces kartik to him. Karthik sees a form in ashwaths hand and asks him what is it about. Ashwath tells them that it's about an inter-college sports meet at Delhi, and he asks Gogi to also join this and put their own college team for cricket competion and that he needs him to win it like good old days. Gogi tells him that he doesn't play cricket anymore and that he is more into boxing now. Also they don't have a team of good players. Karthik tells him that He is an all-rounder and has played cricket for longest times in orphanage. They only had cricket then and used to play that day in and out as they had no other means like TV/Computer for entertainment. Ashwath asks surekha to pull Gogi in and says that ashwath wants to show his Dad what he can do without his support or his name. Surekha forces Gogi puting a cute face and Gogi agrees.

They put a team of theirs. They won initial games to make it to the Final. But at Final they see that umpire is cheating and giving No-balls purposely and not giving out at crucial situations.

Gogi sees the batsman talking with umpire and the next ball itself umpire gives not-out on a run-out throw, thrown by Gogi. Gogi fights with umpire sighting cheating and in a brawl he gets hit by the non-striker with a punch. Gogi in angst boxes him punch after punch and bruises him heavily. Karthik and ashwath runs to stop them but till that time the situation goes worse and the non-striker faints with blood coming out his mouth.

This becomes like a news in the local delhi campuses and everyone starts avoiding Gogi for being violent and un-ethical and also that he gets suspended for 2 months banning entry in the campus further. Veer Ji comes to know about this and he scolds Gogi's mother to put a leash on Gogi. Veer Ji calls on Gogi and asks him to go to ghaziabad and work alongside party workers to know how grass root politics works. He needs to understand politics first to understand Power and that true power lies not in exhibition but it restrain. Gogi finds this as a lecture and without listening it more, he leaves.

He sits in the city play ground where he and Gogi used to Play Cricket. He sits alone there leaning on his car lighting his cigerette. Ashwath and Kartik comes there, ashwath says he knew where Gogi would be. They try to pacify him and make him understand that he needs to control his anger and aggression rather than going berserk. Karthik

Reprimands Gogi that he also doesn't like cheating but they anyway would have won as they were a better team than their opponents. Gogi tells them that he doesn't think he is going to come to college ever again. Everybody hates him. Ashwath tells him that there is other section of campus who likes him, they know that you only reacted against cheating. Ashwath tells him that he has more to him and there is nothing he can't do. Karthik assures Gogi the same. Gogi feels happy about this fact but tells them that he will anyway won't come to college now as he is going ghaziabad and he will later decide accordingly what he feels then.

Devyani Goes to the Coffee shop and drinks coffee after coffee siting there for 3 hrs straight, alone solving MBA entrance papers. She keeps calling ashwath but he doesn't pick the call. She receives his message that he is busy today. Karthik approaches and tells her that she must also eat something than just drinking coffee. Devyani affirms and asks for a sandwich. Karthik sees her involved and asks her what she is preparing for. Karthik tells her about Vedic Maths and how she can do calculations quickly. He had got govt. Scholarships in 4th and 7th grades both times. He says he can offer his High IQ to help if needed. Devyani affirms and karthik explains 2-3 sums to her and then leaves. Devyani after having done with her chapters, she asks Kartik if he could help her further in prepping for MBA. Karthik says yes but he says he won't do it for money. Devyani says she respects his honesty and that she has only friendship to offer. Karthik agrees and smiles. Then Karthik and Devyani spend a good amount of time in studies. They also start spending time other than studies together and develop special feelings for each other. Karthik knows that he cannot match up with his back ground but Devyani affirms him that her Father is very progressive and he won't mind a guy like him marrying her, all he needs to do is get a good job and they are done.

Karthik calls Gogi to tell him about this recent developments but Gogi doesn't pick the call. He then calls surekha to know where

Gogi is. Surekha tells Karthik that Gogi is very much engrossed in the party work, he doesn't even pick her calls. 2 months turn into a year and Gogi in ghaziabad comes to know about the ground reality while prepping for Municipal Elections. How votes are bought, how liquor is sold, How pooling booths are captured, how local people are brainwashed around caste politics. Gogi comes to know a hard fact that cheating is part of the game and all one has to learn is how to cheat and not get caught. Gogi feels vodka in water bottles in the rallies and supplies to the local people like plain water. All the hard work pays off and Jan Shakti Party ward members wons maximum seats in the Municipal Corporation election. Veer Ji feels happy as he didn't expect this result from ghaziabad seats. Gogi returns home after one year and there is a huge celebration at Jan Shakti Party Office. Gogi comes and hugs Veer Ji and He is delighted to see Veer Ji proud of him for the very first time. Ashwath and Karthik too joins him and rejoice in cheer. Veer Ji asks Gogi and his friends to be present at evening Party.

In the party we see all big political and social elites. We see Veer Ji welcoming everyone. Gogi sees Ashwath's Dad touching Veer Ji's feet, so does Surekha's Dad, and even Devyani's Dad. He never knew that Veer Ji has such big impact over his own friend's families too. He thought they are just social buddies. He sees one big entourage of Guards walking around a Senior Politician of Ruling Party, Kishan Singh. He sees accompanying behind them walking Bawana and his mother. Kishan Singh is the only person there who doesn't touch Veer Ji's Feet though he sees him with respect. He sees that Bawana and his Mother touching Veer Ji's feet and Veer Ji blessing them as if he knew them.

Gogi calls one party worker who is his accomplice in ghaziabad about this. He tells Gogi that Laxman Rao, Veer Ji's father was MP under ruling party. But he used to support Jan Shakti party internally providing usefull internal information to Veer Ji. Sadly he died in a cardiac arrest but Veer Ji never forgot Laxman Rao's Contribution. He promised Laxmanrao's wife that he owes a lot to laxmanrao and he will repay all when the time will come. Laxmanrao's Wife didn't ask for any money and she left delhi and went to Chandigarh. She has returned now it seems but he doesn't know what they are doing with Kishan Singh. May be Kishan Singh wants Bawana to join Jan shakti Party because there was one guy who handled north delhi rallies campaigning, it seems this guy could be Bawana.

Gogi gets miffed at this. He observes keenly as to what is happening in the party. Veer Ji calls upon Gogi and tells everyone how happy and proud he is of Gogi that he has worked really hard and that he is thinking of Gogi to make him " Yuva secretary " of Jan shakti Party. Kishan singh praises Veer Ji for his upbringing and tells him afterall he is Veer Ji's blood. But he puts forward Bawana's stretegic mind and campaign design which was a major tool in winning. He thinks Bawana should be rewarded too. He reminds Veer Ji that Bawana's Honesty is non-questionable as his father was a loyal supporter of Jan shakti though being in ruling Party.

Veer Ji gets baffled and tells them that, University elections are ahead, the one who wins, will take the " Yuva Secretary" post of Jan shakti, this is the best way to test the skills and they will also get to learn a lot before upcoming assembly elections which is an important one for everyone of them. Kishan singh smiles seeing this. Gogi and Bawana affirms and exchange cold tension between them.

Karthik and Ashwath helps Gogi in all the strategy and ground campaigning work but they require further funds which Veer Ji refuses to give. He already had allotted equal and enough funds to both Bawana and Him, which is more than enough for a University President. Bawana enjoys a popular support from campus but he too finds it difficult to arrange funds. Gogi enjoys equal support among students with respect to Bawana and both prepare hard for debates, campaigning, posters and agendas. The result gets declared. And Gogi loses to Bawana by very few votes. Gogi congratulates Bawana. Bawana shows no remorse. Bawana says in Gogi's ears that its Jan shakti who has won, it doesn't matter whether it's you or it's me. Gogi doubts bawana's intent here. Bawana celebrates and Gogi's phone rings. His accomplice Rajan tells Gogi that its Kishan Singh, he has provided extra help with funds, He had seen ruling parties Vehicles were at Bawana's place all the time.

Gogi comes to meet Veer ji in anger telling this is cheating, only to find that Kishan Singh is already there. He welcomes Gogi and tells him that ruling party wants to fill their candidate from ghazibad and who better than you to do groundwork for it. To see the fruits after 3 years, one has to start sowing now. Gogi disapproves of this and starts arguing with kishan Singh in a heated manner. Veer Ji reprimands Gogi that Kishan Singh is right and that he needs to still learn a lot before becoming a young leader of 'Jan Shakti' in true sense. Gogi doesn't digest this well and leaves in anger throwing the car keys in Veer Ji's chair. Kishan Singh tells

Veer Ji, "Aap hi ka khoon hai Veer Ji, Gogi ko Gogi Pratap banne se pehle bohot kuch sikhna padega."

Karthik and ashwath sees Gogi leaving the house on his bike, they tty to stop him but he leaves. Gogi goes to surekha's place and calls her to come out. Surekha comes out to see gogi's eyes all red with fuming anger and pain. Surekha takes Gogi in his arms, says nothing and Gogi just sheds his tears.

Gogi goes to Ghaziabad though he doesn't want to. With time, Gogi becomes Gogi bhaiya and becomes a popular youth figure in ghaziabad. Accomplice Rajan and other party workers, tells Gogi how party fund is generated through extortions also. And big businessmen like Gujral pays heavy sums to party and in return the party when comes to power, gives important tenders to these businessmen. This give and take is not just among businessman but teaching institutions to NGO's. Rajan tells Gogi that he himself had extorted money, kidnapped people and what not so many times. Rajan shows Gogi the Gun and Gogi gets surprised. Rajan tells that today they are going to a basti to remove them from their place so that Gujral can build township over there. Gogi too wishes to join Rajan to see how this world works as an observer. Rajan disapproves of this and threatens to tell Veer Ji about this. Gogi snatches the Gun from Rajan and asks him, now what do you think ? Rajan takes him to basti. One strong big leader refuses to leave the basti and abuses Rajan. Gogi starts to talk and leader slaps him in anger, Gogi loses his temper and starts boxing him leaving him bruised heavily. And shouts announcing in anger, " aaj ke aaj saari basti khaali chahiye. " Rajan calls on phone and other workers to come and start working for rehab and tells, " Gogi bhaiya ne kaha hai." Rajan smiles to Gogi and Gogi enjoys the sense of Power this has given him. Soon all the crime related activities which Rajan used to do, Gogi takes complete charge and gets into it. Two-three years passes by and Gogi bhaiya becomes a common threat name in ghaziabad.

In one of the newspapers, when the news of extortion of Big businessmen from Noida comes to picture, Karthik gets disheartened to read this in library. He starts telling Devyani that it is Gogi who has pushed him to become an IPS and now he himself has lost the track. Devyani tells him that he doesn't need to bother. Karthik tells her that how much Gogi has done for him is immeasurable. Its Gogi who has sponsored all his IPS study, he has given him his own place, identity and perhaps everything he could ever ask for as a big brother. He could never repay what he has done for him.

Devyani seems lost in thoughts after listening this. Karthik asks her the reason. Devyani tell him that the marriage rounds are around the corner. And she still doesn't know if he wants to marry her. Karthik tells her that after being an IPS, he can come and talk to her father, before that his father won't approve. Devyani forces him to act fast or else it will be too late. Karthik tells her he can meet his father if she wants but about marriage, he will talk only after he gets selected for IPS, as interview is lined up a month aheada and he needs to study. Devyani hugs him in happiness and tells him to come next weekend evening for a dinner.

The day comes and Karthik meets Mr. Gujral, Devyani's father. Gujral greets Karthik very well and admires the way Karthik has come a long way. Devyani gets happy to see this. While leaving

Karthik, Gujral says very candidly and explains Karthik that he is a nice guy and is not bad as a groom for his daughter. But he has other dreeams for his daughter, he has only one daughter and he wants her to marry in a big house which has a big social and economical value and not just ethical value. Even if he becomes an IPS, he will never be able to provide her the life she desires and he knows it very well. He tells karthik that having come so along, he knows reality very well and he feels he can be practical in life and gives him best wishes. Gujral tells Karthik that he must know the difference between fantasy and reality. And that he should focus on becoming an IPS and forget her daughter and never meet her again in life. On seeing sad face of Karthik when he is leaving, Devyani suspects something and she asks her father, he tells nothing, we were talking about reality and he felt bad about it.

Ashwath calls Gogi and tells him that this is completely not Gogi whom he knew. Crime and politics are two different things. He should concentrate more on Politics and not in crime. He tells Ashwath that he knows nothing about the real world as how it works and he should concentrate on his practice in High court rather than poking his nose in his world. Ashwath tell him that he is getting lost of his real world, he reprimands him to think about Surekha. He hasn't even called her or met her and if he thinks that is he who needs to get the check of reality first.

Rajan tells Gogi about the communist party's interest and tells him that if he needs to increase his power he needs to go beyond ghaziabad and capture other areas like Noida and Gurgaon as well. Rajan tells Gogi that they need to kill the ruling party leader Bhimsen in Gurgaon. Gogi thinks for a while. He doesn't approve of Killing someone. He tells he needs to go home and talk to Veer Ji first.

Gogi comes home after so many years and delighted to see all decoration. Its Veer Ji's 70th Birthday celebration it seems. Gogi goes to Veer Ji, touches his feet but Veer Ji seems disinterested. He tells gogi that he had sent him for other purpose and what he is doing is completely insane. Gogi says to Veer Ji that he knows what he is doing. Kishan singh enters and tells Gogi that he is doing nothing. He doesn't have any idea of how he is embarrassing Veer Ji day after day and that he must stop acting like Veer Ji. If he keeps acting like this he will never become a face of 'Jan Shakti'. Gogi outbursts in anger and yells out his frustration that Veer Ji has a double standard face, he knows all the crime that happens under party funds. Perhaps Veer Ji needs to reflect upon himself and understand what ethics he is talking about. Veer Ji also started as a goon and he wouldn't have been alive today if his father had not taken bullet for him to save him. Gogi's mother listening this from behind comes near Gogi and slaps him hard. She shouts at Gogi and ask him to take his words back and apologize to Veer Ji. Gogi in all red eyes and pain and angst says nothing and leaves the premise. Gogi's mother tries to call him back, Veer ji stops her saying, " You are trying to stop your son, but he is no more that. He is Gogi bhaiya now. "

Gogi calls Rajan and tells him to come to Bhimsen's bungalow directly and take some workers with him. Gogi, Rajan and other workers goes to Bhimsen's bungalow, and being stopped by watchman, he shows his gun. Gogi enters the hall to find bhimsen having dinner with his family. Bhimsen talks with Gogi and pleads he will give him whatever money he wants and that he can even resign from party but he shouldn't kill him. Rajan tells him that what Gogi bhaiya wants he gets it and this time it is his death. Bhimsen tells him that if he wishes to have his power over gurgaon he cannot have it by merely killing him. Rajan shuts bhimsen that he should not talk loud against Gogi bhaiya. Bhimsen smirks and says that He cannot become a Veer ji even he kills 10 bhimsen like him. This triggers Gogi and gogi fires all bullets from his pistol. All family members gets in shock and starts shouting. Rajan fires bullets from his gun and kills other family members.

This creates a big terror around Gurgaon and Gogi bhaiya becomes a big criminal goon by this. Ghaziabad, Gurgaon, Noida all surrounding NCR regions start giving him money. Communist leader and other opposition party members, start making alliances with Gogi. This enrages Veer Ji as he can see Gogi is going against Him and he is losing his Power. The election campaign starts running rounds. Kishan Singh tells him that high command is very unhappy with the Jan Shakti's work as all the young workers work for Gogi bhaiya now and Veer Ji has no power. Kishan Singh tells Veer Ji that Veer Ji needs good powerful alliances and funds if he wants Jan Shakti to file their seat and work for Delhi Constituent assembly or forget the dream of becoming a CM. Kishan Singh tells Veer Ji further that Party has no problem of him becoming a CM one day, infact he is the perfect choice of experience, vision, will and loyalty of 30 years; but he has to do certain ' arrangements '. Veer Ji agrees to this.

Surekha is crying taking pic of Gogi in her hand in her bedroom. His father enters and tells her that Gogi is no more the guy she used to be and that he is now a gangster. There are various cases filed against him and he can never return to the normal world now. There is whole life ahead of her and she can think of her life beyond Gogi. Had her mother been alive, she would never have wanted to live her this way. He apologises to Surekha that he could not love her the way a mother does and has only remained an over protective father. Surekha hugs her father and sobs like a little girl. She tells him that he is world's best Dad. Saying this, Gogi's photo drops from her hand and it lies on the floor as if it has no significance in her life anymore.

Ashwath goes in the court giving statements in Gogi's favour and that there are no evidences only baseless acquisition against him. The court leaves Gogi but ashwath is unhappy about this. Ashwath tells Gogi that there is still a way to it and he can steer his life back to track. Gogi is getting nothing in hand except this fake power, he already has lost family, and now only few have left. He reminds Gogi of he can change people's life as he has Karthik's. Karthik is now an IPS officer and posted in chandausi district of UP. He should also go and meet Surekha. As they go out , Karthik shows him the bike he uses now and tells him that it's his same old bike. Gogi takes the keys, sits on the bike and takes the round in the city, to see the University campus, the cafe he used to sit with surekha, the boxing centre, the playground.

He goes to surekha's house and he finds there is a huge decoration set-up going in. He sees his mother and Veer ji, Kishan Ji and other people there. He is surprised to see Bawana and his Mother too who is taking blessings of Veer Ji. Kishan singh takes mike in his Hand and says that " Politics and Judiciary when go hand in hand, there can only be peace and justice in the society." He announces Bawana to be the next MP candidate from ghaziabad constituency under Jan Shakti and the new emerging face of Jan Shakti and gives mike to Veer Ji. Veer Ji speaks that Bawana is exactly what Laxmanrao,his father used to be; sincere, devoted, educated yet a dynamic fierce leader who can lead, the only difference is that, he was a ruling party leader and Bawna is now the Youth Leader of Jan-shakti Party. And with that he announces his engagement with His old friend and brother Supreme Court Judge's Daughter, Surekha. Bawana takes blessings of Veer Ji and with that exchanges rings with surekha. Surekha is extremely happy and hugs his father after exchanging the ring ceremony. Gogi is shocked to see his entire world shattered in one moment.

He and Rajan sits drinking and he tells him that everything is lost. He could not do a damn little thing. Rajan tells him that why didn't he take stand in his life. Why has he always left undershadow of Veer Ji? He has done everything what veer ji had said and all the power has been given to Bawana including his love surekha. Gogi gets in rage and tells Rajan that his life was best untill he had met Bawana. He is the reason for everything he had lost in his life. He says Rajan that he is going to surrender tomorrow but he needs to do one crime before this. He is going to kill Bawana. He asks for his pistol and keys and leaves. Rajan tells Gogi where bawana is. Bawana is set to leave to chandausi tonight to raise party funds there and he knows where he is resting there. Gogi thanks Rajan and that he has been a good friend to him. Rajan gives a hug and Gogi leaves.

Rajan calls kishan singh and says that Gogi has left for

Chandausi. Kishan Calls the UP home Minister that everything is set and this the right time to act and take revenge of his friend's death, Bhimsen. Home minister arranges for the encounter lead by IPS officer Karthik. Karthik turns in dilema and tells ashwath about it. Ashwath goes to veer ji and tells him about everything. Veer Ji calls Kishan Singh and asks him to stop. Kishan singh tells him that Gogi is going to surrender and tell everything about all the illicit activities and party funds details which is harmful to everyone. Kishan Singh tells that this is not from him but Party High command. All he can do is pass orders and cannot do anything. Veer Ji in all rage throws the phone, Gogi's mother hear this and starts crying. Veer Ji feels helpless and lost as never before. He calls Rajan and tells him that he must leave and stop Gogi and asks ashwath to go behind and he will see what he can do from here.

Gogi enters the place with no one around bawana's house. He easily enters and gets shocked to see that there is no one except for the cars. Many Jan shakti Workers reach the place and make Gogi aware that he needs to go out from Chandausi and that an encounter has been planned against him. No sooner does he say this, one bullet hits the worker and he dies on the spot. This bullet is from Karthik. Gogi is shocked to see this. Gogi and other workers run inside the house and hides. Karthik announces with pain and guilt in his eyes that he needs to surrender and that there is no way. Gogi shouts and says he knows why he had come. To repay his debt. But by killing him, he cannot set himself free. Had he wanted his life he would have given that anyway. Karthik feels helpless. One senior officer comes to Karthik, takes the mic from his hands and shouts again to surrender or there will be consequences. Karthik tries to persuade senior officer that he does not need to kill him.

The senior officer tells karthik that there is no end to it, even if they arrest him and jail him, he is going to die. Gogi is a threat now to all political parties, he should know this reality and he has already learnt all this in IPS training and now he must just do his duty.

One of the workers hit bullet and kills one police officer. The police starts firing again. The fire continues. With time every other worker dies and only Gogi is left. Gogi tries to see through a window and gets hit by one bullet on his shoulder and falls off the ground. He feels his time has come. He calls Veer Ji only to say his last words. He tells Veer Ji that he always wanted to become like him and is sorry that he could never become like him. He says that he will never forget the fact that he had given shelter to his father and gave him his name and treated him as his own grandson. Veer Ji speaks in guilt that he had lost his sight in lieu of power and he says he should have forgotten that. He never had a family, he got one due to his father, Mother and you and come what.may he will always be his grandson. While speaking this one bullet hits his hand and the phone falls down.

Karthik shouts and tries to persuade Gogi one last time. Ashwath arrives at the scene and dares senior Officer to sue him and put a case against everyone and put everyone under bars. The senior officer laughs and just ignores him. Ashwath goes towards karthik and sees a disappointed, helpless friend with a gun in his hand. Rajan tells senior officer that he knows this guest house entry from back yard. He shows them the way and enters from back gate. Rajan leads the way and as he gets inside , Gogi hits a bullet in his head and shouts to Rajan that he deserves this for his betrayal. Karthik moves in from front with another team as he listens heavy firing in the back yard. Gogi is hit by another bullet but this time a bullet straight in his chest.

He sees ashwath and karthik from the window and remembers all the good moments spend with them. He remembers Ashwath's cricket, Karthik's speech. He also remembers surekha, Veer Ji and Mother. Gogi realises his end and looks at the Gun from where it all began. He throws the gun out from the window. He gets all the strength he requires and comes out with all hands up to surrender.

He sees Karthik and Ashwath along with other police officers ahead of him. Gogi keeps on walking and as he sees them he smiles, he looks at Karthik and Ashwath's eyes. And as he smiles his eyes shine. Karthik shouts not to fire but A bullet hits from behind. Followed by other bullets. And in no time Gogi's body is hit by barage of bullets from senior officer and other police behind. Ashwath and Karthik runs in the direction and we see Gogi falling down with the smile intact and blood coming all his body. Seeing this, Karthik stays numb at the place where he is in all state of shock and pain and cries. Ashwath runs to take his body in his lap only to find that Gogi is dead.

Ashwath goes in the court and in the opening statement with the case he has filed against this encounter that what the system has become. He calls IPS karthik for witness. Court listens to everything and adjourns to give another date. Ashwath is disappointed and karthik comes to him that we all know nothing is going to change ever and till what time they will be doing this. Ashwath tells him that perhaps he too knows that but there is no other way to fight.

Karthik and Ashwath shares a glance knowing what they are

doing is for Gogi. They comes out from the court and Karthik sits in his IPS car and Ashwath sits in his regular Car. As ashwath drives along he sees kids playing gully cricket where in a boy is being bullied that its out and he should drop the bat. The boy starts crying and leaves the bat. Ashwath stops the car. He closes his eyes. Removes the spec and the Black court lawyer blazer and comes out of the car. We see ashwath approaching the boys. We see Gogi approaching in the playground to fight for Gogi.

The Proposal

The grandiose Of the hotel Taj tells of its ambiance and the environment with this subtle light as a alluring women enters wearing a lovely red dress From the terraced Restaurant, accompanied by a quiet older man dressed in a casual suit, walks with her arms slipped into his with a sense of pride as they enter the pianist hits the chords greeting the couple. As I watched the two walk by the area is occupied with the couple and families sharing each other's company and enjoying the wonderful atmosphere of this arena. Quite openly emotions can be noted of these fellow guests, as the older couple are indulged into each other whereas the women in the corner is drinking alone, the family discussing their matters at the table with each other. As I was delivering the food to the family I took notice of this women approaching towards the table greeting her, I pulled out the chair for her seeing her smile I greeted her saying Madam you look wonderful today to my surprise just when I glad the man was looking at me with his straight face, continuing and ignoring this fact, taking confirmation for the couple about the shepherd's pie which was the delight for the day I left the table.

The waiter to himself, 'As I kept glancing at their table, I suspected that the women was not interested in this man and was definitely a match she was forced to meet up as her date by, let me guess family'.

Naman, ' Thank you for the time you took care of me, it was your favor that got me through'.

Aashna, ' Let it all pass, Naman, been so long we had a share of these deeds', smiling with an apologetic smear.

Aashna takes out her phone and starts checking her Facebook account, doing the same the man comically looking around, looked at the painting behind her, exclaims Naman, 'That's a monet surely.

Aashna grasps a look, exclaiming it to be nice and expressing a wish as she could stroke a brush like that.

Naman, 'yes I'm sure you can, if you want to', continuing he apologizes to aashna for being late telling her that his mother is having fever, just when his phone rings, goes out to receive it.

She again gets back to her phone when I interrupt her by saying 'Hallelujah'

Aashna, 'What me? ?

With a smirky smile I told her I said hallelujah, as it is one of our special drinking days, as for a beautiful lady like you, a wine on the house, just as I exchanged a glance with the manager.

Aashna, 'Aha, what a day, keep that coming then!

I asked her further if I could get her the special one.

Aashna, 'What is so special about today?

Waiter, 'well didn't you bought that necklace you wearing..?

Aashna, 'How did you know that.?

I exclaimed, 'I couldn't help but notice the price tag.

She starts removing the tag, when I added and it's design, it's one of a kind, which is 'black Sapphire' for what I know, to which she replied as me been a s extraordinary..

As I pour the wine, I asked her if I should pour for her husband..? ?

Aashna, 'we are not married.., trying to smile she tastes the wine, complimenting, 'This is really good'.

As I see the man approaching towards the table, I left with a certain but provoking statement to aashna as, ' he is going to propose you, maybe not today but soon and miss u aren't seem to be prepared for that I suspect.

Aashna is left astounded. Restless the whole night, thinking about the waiters words after Naman proposing her, being restlessness she couldn't help but think about the encounter with the waiter thinking how could a random guy know something like this and know at what stage I really am.

 A day after as the women again comes with his man, seated she gets up from her table, gesturing me to follow her, cornering me she grabbed my arm saying, 'you started something here, I wasn't able to sleep last night, ruined my sober life. how could you even know all this?

Who the hell do you think you are?

To my acknowledgement I replied to the lady what I saw, with no dishonesty.

Miss, 'To begin with I am not a waiter, and I knew this the moment you entered the restaurant with that single look I had, your puzzled eyes, but I might say this as you should think and rationally respond to the situation that is coming you way, GOOD LUCK!

Disrupting the conversation with her, saying that my manager is looking towards us and I should be back, I left.

As I run to complete my chore, she heads back to her table.

I went up to the bar for a drink, poured a glass for myself.

To my notice, the rest of the evening came to be in a certain stillness as the lady drifted in her own thoughts, whereas the man tried a couple of vain attempts to start up a conversation, when his phone rings and goes out to take his call.

Aashna looking pale and lost to whatever happened, thinking about the waiter.

Just when the guys came in and proposed Aashna on his knees, she looked at me, just when I finished my drink with a shrug, our eyes meet for a second as I take off my dinner jacket and put my tuxedo overcoat, she comes up straight towards me, leaving Naman behind, who is left dismayed and disgusted as he was left on his knees by Aashna to his shock.

Meanwhile, I leave the restaurant and crossed the road, light my cigarette, glaring at the beautiful view of the sea.

Aashna comes and stands besides him, Asked, ' Who are you..? ?

Atharva (waiter) my name is Atharva, 'I'm an actor and this was the part for my next film which I was processing'.

Atharva with a calm and pleasant demeanor stands and takes a puff.

Aashna, ' thank you, but still I didn't know if you have saved my life or spoiled my date, here. As she asks for the puff, and smiles, feeling surprised and full of wonder at the moment.

Atharva takes a glance at her, just smiles.

SIMMI

That night it all started, the feeling of being numb screaming inside, like it all ended with the blink of an eye. Sharman a 27 years old man standing in his balcony holding his phone looking miserable and sad, just when his friend fatty comes up looking at his face commenting about the arrival of his Grandfather who was about to come and meet Sherman, clearing up the mess that was their room in, they went and opened the door to welcome sherman's grand father denoting him as dadu greeting him sherman gives him a hug. My dove is with dadu taking care of him opens up his bag to give dadu his medicines, when dodoo exclaims of him taking medicine at this age with warm water is beneficial. madhav leaves with fatty to the kitchen to get water for dadu. Who start up a conversation dadu comments on sherman's haircut telling him he looked like a movie star jitender to which Sherman replies that he had too because of office and work. Just as dadu asks Sherman about the condition of Chandigarh sharmans phone drinks which he deliberately rejects and continues to chat with dadu again A few seconds later his phone rings again and then dadu insist on going but soon Sherman picks up his phone tells the dadu to sit and he himself walks out to attend the call, dadu with his keen observation notices the tension of sharman's face and gives a keen look towards him as if he knew that something is wrong. Meanwhile fatty tries to make small talk with madhav in the kitchen, fatty predicts and tells madhav to smoke out if he wants to when madhav asked for a lighter But instead he wanted to light the stove. Fatty continues to talk asking if madhav belongs from Rajasthan and then predicting about him as for having camels and that the survival capacity of the people belonging from that region have, fatty continues to his disguise saying you must be banned as madhav don't wear a turban or have a mustache either. Madhav who was getting annoyed by fatty gives fatty a look and walks out with a glass of water for dadu , dadu while taking his medicine tells fatty that madhav is quite strict when it comes to his medicines and never let him forget them. Fatty telling dadu that it's good to take medicines on time to which dadu continues to say with a slight gesture that medicine is good but one can take other things as well for relief. Sharman enters with a long face and asks fatty if his room is ready and to take dadu there and asks madhav and fatty to adjust to sleep in the hall for the night. Sharman with his serious demeanor tells dadu that his flight is at 10:30am and he has to get going at 8:30 as he will to leave for his office and the airport is a bit far from apartment. Dadu listening to all this catches his hand

and makes him sit down, turning up towards fatty and madhav saying were you talking about having drinks fatty, blinking at madhav, dadu tells him to take out his whiskey bottle. Preparing each one short for everyone and starts to talk when fatty reveals by mistake why Sharman is being uncomfortable, as because of his girlfriend simmi, dadu turning Sharman to ask what has happened, Sharman with sad tensed voice says, 'she wants to go Japan, grandpa, even through she do not like Japan.' Fatty tries to make the air light but instead cracks a lame joke, after which dadu indicates sharman to go out in the balcony, and sharman leaves with his glass. Dadu follows Sharman to the balcony to talk, looking at sharman sad dipped face, he asks him why he even want simmi not to go Japan as she will be back after a few years. 'What will I do dadu?' sharman

'You'll wait' dadu, he continues to share his own love story to sharman, telling him how when he was 13 he met his 1st love in Shimla and then I told her upfront that I'm going to marry you' although I didn't even knew at that time that she wasn't from Shimla, but I kept hope and waited till I turned 23 years old and met her again. At least you know her address. Sharman, 'I know dadu but things are different now and much complicated, which wasn't the case at your time, and she do not even want to go Japan, she is just going because she want to get married.'

Dadu, with whom 'Joy Mukherjee' with a laughter in his voice. Sharman with a bit of a smile in his face tells dadu that simmi wanted to get married to him only. Dadu, 'then what's the problem?' before sharman could speak fatty enters a bit drunk saying to them no problem, as they met on tender and he can meet more people, sharmam explains dadu about this dating app, and diverts the topic to dadu's love story asking him if he met the girl? Dadu, 'No, I did not, but I had faith that I was going to meet her someday, in those times waiting was like a passion and a challenge, going on about what he did and how he started acting and one day she came back when her father opened this new shop at hall road and that's when she came to invite me for the celebrations.

Tell me about simmi – dadu, there is a bit of longing and a sense of oneness when when sharman started talking about simmi telling dadu , things and he whereabouts, and how they met in a club, suddenly fatty interrupted sharman by saying the word tender, sharman with his agitated voice completed by saying- 'they met on tender and talked about meeting in the club, with the same emotion sharman told fatty to leave from there, but fatty started reading simmi profile on his phone and jokes with sharman about her status as being changed to single on facebook. Sharman snatches the phone from fatty giving him a annoyed look, dadu and fatty awarded laughing and they told fatty to go inside and to not add to his troubles. Dadu started talking to sharman on a serious note about the problem, asking the exact thing that bothered him to which sharman with a deep voice and a heavy heart told marriage is the main problem, saying that it is too early for him to settle, that he has career goals, he wants to buy his own house and then he can think about getting married. Dadu making him understand, why is he putting conditions over things, for being married, being happy, and why postpone your joy and happiness for the future. Don't do that. Sharman, dadu. Sharman, 'I just want 1 and a half year, I'll have some money, will borrow some and take loan, there will be my house and a stable job and then things will get easier and life will be good and easy, besides if she ever wanted to go then she should have gone 3 years back, she refused and now a of a sudden she accepted the job , why because dadu, I think she is not serious about our relationship or me. I don't care let her go, I don't think this is meant to be.'

Sharman looking does with disappointment when dadu tries to tell sharman about the things people generally do, when faced with difficulty and challenges, we run and move on, ' I too went through the same before my Marriage I was broke, and her father was planning to get her married someplace else, for me at that point in my life there was nothing left but to run and to leave everything and go, Sharman, ' what did you do then?' just when dadu was about to anwere Sharman madhav voice came form inside , as fatty and madhav was drunk completely and enjoying the music, madhav was singing.

A memory of simmi flashed in front of Sharman and as he glances simmi he closes his eyes, then looking at his phone screen to their picture together. Dadu too shares the picture of his love with Sharman, looking at his grandmother picture, with contempt in his face says to dadu what's the point now you were not there when dadi needed you the most, remembering some situations, accuses his grandfather (dadu) For not being there and the tension that created between him and his father won't be there at first place.

Dadu, ' your father never understood my limitations and circumstances, I had to go on a business trip for 10 days, the same time your grandmother fell ill, and before I could return back, every person's life is a set of different stories, I won when I met her and got defeated the moment I lost my wife and mt children. I wish that time also the technology was that fast and we could have cellphones and apps, well its enough for today, just for the love story, let's keep the pain and jilted lovers story for some other day. Sharman with a fake smile tells dadu why leave that part of the story, as he is in the same state, Sharman, 'simmi is going and there nothing I can do about it, I'm here sitting drunk.'

'Simmi is angry on you because you are running away.' Dadu. Listening to this, Sharman with the tears in his eyes turns towards dadu with lots of questions. Dadu goes on saying that it is the right time for you to take responsibility and fulfil it. And all at once Sharman's questions seems to go and there is a sense of acknowledgement in his eyes to do something now. Soon after realizing this fact and the true meaning of what his grandfather had told him he remembered all the things and the solution dadu gave to him, the very next morning he went to simmi's house with everyone, going inside and standing infront of simmi's door and a bit nervous of what he might say, as soon as she opens the door he begins to tell simmi, ' simmi you don't like the job and Japan as well , please stay here' don't go please. Simmi, 'looking down and listening to sharman, what will I do here then?' sharman bend down as if he is going to propose when simmi stops him, he stand sup saying that he bend down just to tie the lace. They both laugh and sharman continue to express his feelings to simmi , telling her that he is ready for everything and requests her to cancel her tickets. After a brief pause simmi says 'she haven't booked the tickets, telling sharman he is not the only one smart here…!

Sharman face lights up with a smile and they both hug each other, while hugging simmi notices the dadi standing outside, asking sharman about him who is standing with fatty..? When sharman exclaimes that he is the "coolest daadu" !!

Sharman, 'when things happen we are responsible as dadu was responsible for what happened with my grandmother but he knew this fact and he is the one who today made me understand about the responsibility and not to run from them, he has his story, his own truth and he has suffered a lot but no one else better then him knows the fact of what he did and he has his own realization.

Cover Story

"I have been observing from quite some time that you always carry this book with a bearded man on the cover picture whenever you come to this fort. What's the name of this book ?" asked Aanshi with a smirk on her face.

Vickey replies, "It's called 'Cover Story'."

"Wow! I have heard a lot about this book. The writer minted a lot of money through it. After all, it's a bestseller! I was quite intrigued by the book but couldn't read it because of time constraints/ busy schedule. Why do you keep this book with you all the time, haven't you read it for like more than a hundred times! Are you a fan ?"

"I think I should tell a story to answer your questions... Mmm, a love story!" replied Vickey.

"It's ironic , how you could come up with the idea of telling a love story while enduring a heartbreak yourselves!" retorted Aanshi.

Vickey answered, "Actually, it's about a failed love story of

India's most celebrated motivational speaker and a Best Selling Romantic Novelist."

Aanshi replied in a teasing manner, "A failed love story! That was expected from you. Also, a motivational speaker! It kind of rings a bell in my head. I have read a few articles about him I guess."

"You must listen to the story till the end to know about it", said Vickey.

Okay, okay! nodded Aanshi .

The story is about two personalities. One of them motivates others to keep himself going while the other writes romantic novels to forget love completely.

Vickey started telling the story, "It's a beautiful winter morning. A thirty-year-old strikingly handsome man, Vikrant Pratap is delivering a speech in a picturesque open auditorium at the Dehradun literature festival. Renowned writers, journalists & various other prominent personalities from all over the country have gathered at the venue to witness this event. After concluding his speech he leaves for the canteen. Arundhati Singh, a 45 year old, graceful woman approached him. She is a renowned novelist for your - 'FYI.'

Are you talking about "The Arundhati Singh"! The famous writer of the book that you are holding in your hand? Exclaimed Aanshi.

"Yes! I am talking about her.

Don't interrupt. I am trying to tell a story! "

"Okay okay!" muttered Aashi while gesturing her hands into closing her mouth with an imaginary zip.

Vickey explains, "Arundhati is one of the best romantic novelists in the country. All her novels have been listed as bestsellers. She has written three consecutive best-selling books."

Aashi interrupts by saying,

"Even two of the books written by her are ready to be adapted for a feature film.

OR

"Even two feature films are based on the novels written by her."

Vickey shushed Aanshi and continued his story,

"Arundhati admitted to Vikrant that she really liked the motivational speech and was quite impressed by his choice of words. 'How amazing was it to witness the whole auditorium filled with energy, enthusiasm and positive vibes. The audience was SPELLBOUND and I sighted some rare MAGICAL moments. You give a ray of hope to people. You can boost the morale of the people even in crisis and make them realise that this is not the end of the world'.

Both of them met formally and then started a conversation about their professional journey. As their conversation deepened, Arudhanti asked Vikrant about his love life. Vikrant was hesitant at first. He denied it initially but later on, he revealed his real story on the condition of confidentiality.

He started telling her about his love story while reminiscing about his past. He told her that he met a gorgeous/lovely girl named Smriti Singh during his final year in post-graduation. He used to work as an assistant for a well-known speaker at that time. Life was good, both of them used to meet and hang out. She was pursuing MBA and wanted to launch her own start-up company abroad. They became good friends. They shared similar interests. Both of them were hodophilias. They even started travelling together. He started falling for her and assumed she felt the same. After a year, one day he planned a proposal at their favourite hangout spot at a fort. She rejected his proposal saying "he was just a good friend to her."

He was miserable for a few days. He felt embarrassed and remorseful. He tried to convince her that it happened by mistake and he shouldn't have done it so early. He tried his best to make things normal. He still wanted to be friends with her because he really loved her. But nothing worked out for him. She blocked him & left the place. He just wanted to meet her once & convince her that it was a mistake. But he never got a chance to do so.

After a few days, he went to an event. He was heartbroken, emotionally drained, and was dejected. Suddenly he saw a few people outside the seminar hall rushing towards a balcony where a person was trying to commit suicide. Vikrant went there and came to know that he was depressed and was fed up with his life. He started comforting him and motivated him through the stories that he heard from his boss. The guy listened to the story calmly and finally came down. He hugged Vikrant tightly and offered him to start his seminar.

From that point in his life, Vikrant secluded himself. He cut off his ties from everything that held him back. He deleted his old social media accounts, changed his phone number and email. He started working day in and day out. He transformed into a completely different person. He discarded all his old clothes and replaced them with formal business attire and transformed his wardrobe. He would always wear a tuxedo or formal attire. He started working out seriously. He even started dating and exploring the world. He kept himself busy and got his life well-organized/ in order.

After three years, Vikrant became a renowned successful man. His physical appearance did change a little bit. He grew a big beard & sported a perfect coiffed hairstyle. He got engaged to his current girlfriend but all of a sudden one day he saw Smriti with someone. For a moment he felt alive and peaceful. He realized what he has missed over the years. He has become a clockwork monster, continuously working like a machine all day long. In his continuous efforts to chase goals, he forgot to live and enjoy life. He worked so hard to keep himself busy and in an attempt to forget everything, he kept his real self in cover/ concealed his real self.

He followed Smriti & realized that she had been married recently. She ran a food business with her husband and was very happy.

He dismissed his plans to marry his fiancé, he apologized to her for everything, convinced her that why he is not really happy doing all these and went back to his normal life. After a few days, he is invited to be the star speaker of the Dehradun literature festival. And hence, he is here sharing his story with Arundhati.

They became emotional. He reiterates that he is not the same person that he was three years ago. He is neither truly happy nor dejected. He realized that this is how life is meant to be. He still loves her. He tried his best to win her love but never got a chance. He hopes that someday something better would happen to him. He opined that , 'Everyone does not have a perfect romantic story like those beautiful stories written by you'. Not everyone is blessed by love in this life.'

Hearkening his story, Arundhati was all verklempt. She started sharing her love story.

She met a senior named Rameez in the first year of college at Delhi University in 1993./ She was studying at Delhi University in 1993 when she met a senior named Rameez in the first year of her college. This super amazing person was a student leader. They started hanging out. They would often meet each other and have beautiful moments together. That was the happiest time of her life. Every moment with him seemed to be filled with joie de vivre. She never felt the same before & after this. He used to make her happy. He could even make her joyous in the unpleasant situations. She would feel uninhibited, free and safe with him. There was never a dull moment with him. They fell head over heels in love with each other. They were so much in love that they started dreaming about their future together.

Then, she recalled the 'black day' of her life. There was a widespread political unrest in the country. Rameez was leading the protest. Suddenly a riot began and many people were killed. Several buildings were destroyed and vehicles were set on fire. She never saw him again. She doesn't know what has happened to him.

It is even more painful for her because she doesn't know whether he is still alive or dead. Even his family and friends did not receive his body.

She went into depression for two years. Then just like any other woman of an Indian orthodox family, she was pressurised to get married. She married a gentleman named Raman who was a professor at Delhi University. This man tried everything to make her happy (like a true lover). But she couldn't feel the same even after trying her best. She was lacking spirit. She was alive but not living. In a few years, they were blessed with two lovely kids. It was the only reason they were together.

One day their relationship came to an end. She broke down into tears. Unable to repress her emotions, she blurted out the truth that she was unhappy with their marriage and confessed to Raman, 'Once I was a lively, bright student...Now what...what the hell I have become! Living like a housewife.... having two kids, every day is same - dull and mechanical. My life is a mess, I simply exist without having any dreams & goals. I can not live like this anymore.'

He understood that she was unhappy with their marriage. He promised that he would never pressurize her and would never compel her to talk. He would take care of the kids. They started living separately in the same house for kids. He silently supported her in every possible way. He moved heaven and earth to make her happy. They hardly talked to each other for twelve years. Then she began reading and writing novels, just to forget some memories. She started writing fiction to cover something real.

"No one has a perfect story. All of us conceal our sad stories behind our masked realities". Sometimes she feels bad for Raman, she thinks that she is not meant for him. He is too good for her and she thinks that she doesn't deserve him. He loves her selflessly. He devoted his entire life to her.

Vikrant tries to convince Arundhati to give a chance to Raman. What happened to her first love Rameez was unfortunate but Raman is her second chance to seek love and she has not realized it yet. She should give herself a chance to love him. It's not necessary that every love story or feeling should be the same. Each & every person is uniquely different. The person who truly loved her and stood by her side for more than twenty five years, maybe that's supposed to be her true love. What else does she need?

Arundhati gets carried away by her emotions. She then smiles and asks permission from Vikrant to write a novel inspired by his story. Vikrant signed his consent on one condition that she should meet Raman first & live the rest of her life happily with him. Both of them felt relieved after sharing their stories. They said their goodbyes and left for their flights with a promise to meet each other soon.

Arundhati straightaway goes to meet Raman at the college classroom. They had an emotional breakdown. They started crying.

She wrote a novel based on Vikrant's story & published it within a month. It became the best selling novel of that time.

The title of the novel was 'COVER STORY'

(The failed love story of India's most celebrated motivational speaker). She meticulously penned the tiny details like- how Vikrant still visits the same fort during the last Sundays of every month. The book was launched with Vikrant's photo on the cover.

Smriti goes on a business trip. She goes to a bookshop with her friend. Where they saw a bookstall with numerous copies of the best selling novel "The Cover story". Her friend was quite excited to read the bestseller, so she buys it. Smriti scans the book closely & took one for her as well. She reads the novel in isolation and gets overwhelmed while reading it.

Vikrant was sedulous like earlier. But something has changed in him. He seems to be happier. Now he is sporting a clean-shaven look, and donning colourful clothes once again, like before/ like he used to earlier. There is a complete transformation in his looks.

Arundhati spends quality time with her family. She is happy and is going out with Raman.

One fine evening, Vikrant was at the same fort peacefully watching the beautiful sky changing it's colours , relishing the sunset. Suddenly, someone called him from behind. He was amazed by the mannerisms of the stranger who called him because her way of speaking was very similar to his.

Aanshi, an architecture student came to the fort for the research work. Vikrant liked her and initiated a conversation about architecture."

"But i have never met this bearded guy Vikrant!" countered Aanshi.

Really! replied Vickey. "let me continue the story,

She didn't recognize him nor did he mention any details about him. He asked her to help him with research and......"

With a sudden realisation Aashi shrieked, "Oh.... You...you are Vikrant! The Vikrant! motivational speaker." She exclaimed in disbelief.

Anyway, how would I reckon it! You never motivated me! You only talked about your heartbreaks and that too...to a point that i had to motivate you!

Vikram continues amusingly, "hahaha, Yes.

Vikrant lied to Aanshi that he is working with the archaeological department to restore the fort."

Aanshi scoffs him saying,

"Hmm. His lies were hilariously busted by me. Because you know nothing about architecture, Vickey Pratap aka Vikrant Pratap! "

Every love story is not perfect, it shouldn't be perfect. Life gives a second chance to everyone. "Never cover your second chance, never cover your real self."